R2
Cute!

He would have noticed her anywhere...

As she reached down to adjust a sandal, his gaze moved to her rising skirt. If she bent down one more inch...

Jackson fumbled with his tie. What was wrong with him? Gina swayed as she stood up, looking pale, and he felt like a heel. He was supposed to be helping her! He cleared his throat and moved to pour her a glass of water.

She sat on the edge of his sofa, and her skirt hitched up again. "Sorry to be so much trouble. I'm sure you're busy and—"

She stopped short and stared at him in open surprise as he gulped down the water he'd poured. Realizing what he'd done, he quickly filled a new glass and passed it to her.

"It's awfully hot in here."

He lifted his palm and pressed it against her forehead. "You're burning up. I'm going to call a doctor. We have to do something for you."

"No! But...there is one thing that would help."

"Name it."

"If you wouldn't mind," she said, "I'd be much cooler with my blouse off."

Dear Reader,

I don't know about you, but my family and I can't pass by a fountain without throwing a coin in and making a wish.

Gina, Libby and Jessie are just like me. When they find themselves at the world-famous Trevi Fountain, they send out their wishes for happiness on those gilt-edged coins they toss. But sometimes, no matter what we *say* we want, our hearts know what we *truly* need....

So it is for Gina, here in Debbi Rawlins's IF WISHES WERE...HUSBANDS and for Libby in Karen Toller Whittenburg's IF WISHES WERE... WEDDINGS (October) and for Jessie in Jo Leigh's IF WISHES WERE...DADDIES (November).

I'm happy to say that some of my wishes have come true.... Let's see how it works out for Gina, Libby and Jessie in the Three Coins in a Fountain miniseries.

Happy reading!

Debra Matteucci
Senior Editor & Editorial Coordinator
Harlequin Books
300 E. 42nd St.
New York, NY 10017

If Wishes Were...
HUSBANDS

DEBBI RAWLINS

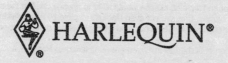

HARLEQUIN®

TORONTO • NEW YORK • LONDON
AMSTERDAM • PARIS • SYDNEY • HAMBURG
STOCKHOLM • ATHENS • TOKYO • MILAN • MADRID
PRAGUE • WARSAW • BUDAPEST • AUCKLAND

This is for Joe and Terry Quattrone.
With love and admiration.
Thank you for believing in me.

ISBN 0-373-16741-5

IF WISHES WERE...HUSBANDS

Copyright © 1998 by Debbi Quattrone.

Chapter One

Gina Hart was running out of bribes. How could anyone not like Godiva chocolates? She gave the dour-faced maid a suspicious glance before setting the gold box down on the stone urn sitting near the door to Nick's villa. The candy had probably melted, anyway. But Smiley here wouldn't know that. Unless she'd seen Gina hiding in the bushes under the hot Italian sun for nearly an hour. Gina had almost given up, too, and decided it wasn't worth surprising Nick for his birthday after all. She'd been about to ring the bell when the maid had come to the door to accept a milk delivery.

Although she generally didn't judge people so quickly, Gina didn't much like this woman whose oddly amused black beady eyes stared back at her. There was something unnatural about not liking chocolate. And besides, the woman was guilty of another grievous fault. She was thin.

Sighing, Gina smoothed the peach linen skirt, wrinkled from the long transatlantic flight, down the too-generous curves of her hips. She lifted her chin. Wouldn't Sourpuss here be surprised if Gina ended up being mistress of the manor?

Uneasy, Gina promptly lowered her chin when she

realized she was getting ahead of herself. She and Nick'd had a few intense dates, but he hadn't exactly popped the question, nor had she expected him to. And even if he had, Gina honestly didn't know what she'd say. To her disgust, she'd been preoccupied with the idea of marriage since turning thirty last week. And she'd damn well better knock it off if she didn't want to scare Nick silly.

"You sure you don't speak English?" Gina asked the woman with exaggerated slowness, as if drawing out the words would magically translate her English to Italian.

Gina's grandmother was from Italy, and had lived in a village just outside of Rome. And now she wished she'd paid attention when the stern older woman had tried to teach her language to Gina and her sisters. But kids of their generation growing up in Brooklyn had no use for the ways or language of the old country.

Folding her hands together, the woman slowly shook her dark head, her pinched gaze leaving Gina's face only long enough to flick a disapproving look at the short hem of the peach skirt. Actually, she kind of reminded Gina of Nana. She wore her hair in the same tight ebony bun, and her plain face looked as though it had never been blasphemed by makeup.

"Okay, let's see." Gina let the heavy brown leather bag slide down from her shoulder to her elbow while she rooted through it in search of some other kind of payola. She pulled out a gold pen and held it up, slowly, enticingly waving it under the woman's hawkish nose.

The maid's mouth puckered up to match the rest of her frowning face.

"For goodness' sake, it's a Cross pen, and I only want you to let me in unannounced," Gina muttered, giving the woman a dark look before she continued digging. The bag was too crowded, and to make room for her rummaging, she withdrew the special bottle of Bordeaux she'd picked up in Paris.

From under her lashes, she saw the maid's eyes light up.

Gina did a double-take. "Oh, no, not the Château Lafite." At the woman's blossoming smile, Gina's shoulders sagged. "Come on. Don't do this to me."

"*Si.*" The maid extended her wrinkled hand.

"Damn. Damn. Damn." Gina started to surrender the wine. Without hesitation, the woman's fingers closed around the neck of the bottle. Gina held on for a moment longer, loathe to give up the expensive Bordeaux she'd bought to toast her and Nicky's future. The maid yanked, and a brief tug-of-war ensued before Gina finally gave in.

Nick had once said nothing ever surprised him. Gina wanted to be the one to change that. And the only thing standing in her way was this oversize pit bull. Oh, well, giving up the wine for that chance wasn't that big a deal, she thought with a sigh. She gave the impressive exterior of the huge villa another long sideways glance. Nick was loaded. He probably had tons of better stuff to drink in his own private wine cellar.

He wouldn't care that she came with nothing. Just herself, in the short, tight peach skirt he loved so much, along with the body-hugging white scoop-neck T-shirt. One of the things she liked about him was that although he had oodles of money, he wasn't a stuffed shirt. Plus, he still worked as a pilot. And he was nice as well as charming.

Working as a transatlantic courier for the past four years, she'd met lots of men, many of them pilots, most of them arrogant and self-absorbed. Not Nicky. Even her grandmother would approve of him. Then maybe she'd quit giving Gina decks of Old Maid cards for her birthday.

Gina's determined gaze rested on the maid's bowed head as the woman studied the bottle's label. Gina cleared her throat, and the woman looked up with a frown.

"Well, excuse me for bothering you, you heartless little swindler," Gina said with a smile. When the woman merely reacted with a quizzical lift of her brows, clearly not understanding, Gina added, "You never would have gotten away with this in my Brooklyn neighborhood." Her grin broadened as she made an international motion with her hand, asking entrance. "Know that, you weasel?"

The woman gave her a small begrudging smile back, and pushing the door wider, she stepped aside.

Although the outside of the villa was understandably battered from age and inclement weather, the inside stole Gina's breath. Sunlight glistened off crystal chandeliers and sprayed rainbows of color across the white marble-tiled floor. Original paintings hung on the walls. At least Gina assumed they were originals. Men like Dominic Carlucci owned nothing but the best.

"*Signorina?*" The maid gestured toward the curved staircase. From the second floor, music floated down. It was an opera Gina had heard before but couldn't identify. People from Manhattan went to operas and ballets. Back in Brooklyn, Gina considered going to the park and watching the street performers a social event.

The thought made her a little queasy. Of course, she'd come a long way from her Brooklyn roots. Traveling internationally for the past few years had taught her a lot. Still, Nick was from a different world....

She swallowed back the sudden misgiving forming a tangled gob of nerves in her throat, straightened her spine and started climbing the stairs. She was Gina Hart, after all, street-smart if not book-smart, outgoing, funny....

Her thoughts stumbled as she neared the top step. The music got louder and her pulse quickened. What else had her grandmother hammered into her thick skull? Gina needed all the positive reinforcement she could get right now. As impulsive as she was, she'd never done anything like this before—showing up unannounced, baggage in hand, thousands of miles away from home.

Either she was the biggest sap in history, or...Gina smiled to herself. She was worrying for nothing. Nick was going to be thrilled she'd surprised him.

She paused at the second-floor landing and glanced down at the maid. Her evil little smile showed white teeth that Gina fervently hoped got good and stained by the confiscated red wine. Nodding graciously to the woman, she held her head higher and walked toward the music.

She couldn't wait to see Nick's face. The entire grueling trip would be worth it when she did. Normally, she took two-week breaks between courier jobs to shake the exhausting jet lag, but she hadn't been able to wait to see Nick.

Pausing outside the closed door, she combed her fingers through her hair and fluffed out her bangs. When she ran her tongue across her lips, they felt a little grainy, so she slipped a compact out of her bag, licked then wiped off the blotched color and swept on some fresh pale pink gloss. After adjusting the waistband of her skirt to make sure the seams lined up properly, she inhaled deeply, sucked in her stomach, smiled and pushed open the door.

Looking tousled and sexy as hell, Nick sat up in his bed. He was shirtless, his tanned chest a work of art against the white satin sheets.

Gina's pulse did an appreciative jig. "Hi, Nicky," she said in her sultriest voice. "Happy birthday."

"Gina?" He looked only mildly surprised. And not entirely happy. His gaze shifted to the left.

Out of the corner of her eye, she saw movement at the same time she heard a disbelieving feminine voice say, "Nick?"

Gina's head whipped around. A short blonde was huddled in the corner, hugging herself, her large eyes registering the shock Gina was beginning to feel clear down to her aching, too-cramped toes. Several feet from her, a dark-haired woman was spilling out of a skimpy lavender negligée. Upon seeing Gina, her eyes flashed fire and she threw up her hands, rattling off a barrage of Italian.

Slowly, Gina returned her gaze to Nick, dread making her tongue feel like a two-pound knockwurst and rendering her totally incapable of speech. No need to jump to conclusions, she tried to tell herself. There was probably a perfectly reasonable explanation....

A scuffling noise came from the window near the bed and the drawn curtains billowed suddenly. Nick straightened. The blonde gasped.

Out of the yards of gossamer fabric stepped a red-headed woman. Her smile unerringly found Nick, then faded as her gaze slowly swept first the blonde, then the dark-haired woman, and finally Gina. The redhead blinked.

"Nick?" the blonde repeated, her voice barely a whispered plea.

"Nick?" Gina's demand wasn't quite so charitable.

"Nick?" the redhead added.

The woman in the negligée shrieked something else in Italian.

He didn't even look embarrassed. He sat up straighter with a grin on his face that was only marginally sheepish. "What a surprise," he said. "How nice of you all to drop in."

"Drop in?" Gina's shoulders sagged and her bag slid down to the floor with a thud. "Drop *in?* I came all the way from Los Angeles. Three planes. No sleep. And I turned down two courier jobs. I did *not* just drop in."

"Oh, Nick," the blonde said, her wide blue eyes looking wounded. "I told *everyone* we were going to get married."

Married? To the blonde? Anyone could see she wasn't his type, Gina thought peevishly as she eyed the petite woman. She was too wholesome, or something. Gina let out a pent-up breath, and with it, the silly pettiness that threatened. In spite of her own anger and humiliation, she felt sorry for the blonde. She looked young and terribly unsure right now. As if Gina was feeling any more confident.

Sighing softly, she eyed the brunette. The woman had an impressive set of breasts, which made Gina stand up straighter and throw her shoulders back. That didn't help much. She was mildly consoled that the woman didn't look like the forgiving type, and Gina figured Nick was already out of luck with her.

The redhead was something else altogether, Gina decided as her gaze wandered over the woman and her expensive, well-cut suit, the reserved way she held her-self. Gina swallowed. This woman was more his type.

"So it's like this, is it?" the redhead asked, her voice admirably cool, her demeanor poised as she folded her arms across her chest. "It was all a game?"

"It was never a game," Nick said.

"You meant everything you said?" the redhead asked.

"Yes."

"Oh, brother." Gina threw up a hand and groaned.

She thought the blonde might have growled, but Gina's gaze was glued to the other woman and the silent battle she was waging with Nick. Her eyes were locked with his in combat, and the tension was so thick a buzz saw couldn't have penetrated it. And Gina knew in that instant she didn't have a chance with Nick. Not that she wanted one, the pig.

"So you love all of us?" the redhead asked.

"*Si,* Jessie, I love you all."

She stared at him in shocked disbelief, slowly shaking her head as her eyes met Gina's.

"I can't believe I told everyone we were going to get married," the blonde muttered, sounding outraged. "What should we do now?"

"It is four to one," Gina said, shrugging. "We could take him."

Jessie sighed, a slight smile briefly lifting her lips. "I saw a small bistro just down the road. I imagine they serve liquor there. It is Rome, after all. I think I'm going to get well and truly drunk." She glanced at the blonde, the brunette, then back to Gina. "If you'd care to join me?"

"Please stay, *cara mia,*" Nick said. "I can explain everything."

Gina stared at him, anger battling humiliation inside her, grating her emotions so raw she wanted to bolt. The guy was too much. Was he that confident or clueless? No, not clueless. Not Nick. How could she have been so stupid as to be taken in by him? She was smarter than this. What the hell was wrong with her?

Pilots. She shook her head.

She knew better. From now on, she was staying away from them. Not just pilots, though, but men like Nick who had more power and charm than they had a right to, and who used those weapons like disposable paper towels. She sighed. Maybe her brothers were right. She'd be better off sticking to her own kind…a nice blue-collar guy.

She shook her head again. She really should have known better. Nick was out of her league. Men like him wanted nothing but the best. That did not include a girl from Brooklyn.

"Count me in," she told Jessie. "I could use a shot or two."

"I'll go," the blonde said. "I've never been drunk before, but this seems like the perfect time to get that way."

The brunette only stared, her arms crossed, her murderous glare skewering Nick. Maybe she didn't understand English.

Oh, hell. Gina cringed. Maybe she was his wife.

Gina swallowed, then forced a smile. Jessie smiled back, and the three of them turned toward the door. This entire scene was like a really bad sitcom. Except there wasn't a damn thing funny about it.

"TO TAR AND FEATHERS!"

Jessica lifted her wineglass and clinked it against

Libby's, then Gina's. "Here, here."

"Ditto," Libby said, nodding enthusiastically before she took another sip of wine. "Hot tar."

Gina grinned at her companions. She was proud of them. "You're really getting the hang of this revenge scheme. I can't decide which one I like the best!" Originally she'd had to come up with the honey and ants, a short walk out of a 747 at thirty thousand feet—without a parachute—and now the tar and feathers. But it had been Jessica's idea to rent a billboard outside La Guardia airport and post a Wanted picture. She sighed with admiration. The woman had real class.

"I can't believe I spent all that money to come here," Libby said. "I don't think I can afford a billboard."

Jessica and Gina both nodded in sympathy. It was obvious that Libby was the youngest and least experienced of the three. She was also gorgeous, and Gina bet few men would turn her down. No wonder she thought Nick had really intended on marrying her.

"I spent a lot of money to get here, too," Jessie said, and sighed. "It just goes to show that you can't trust them. Not ever. Men are louses." Jessie frowned. "Lice?"

Gina snorted. "You've got that straight. Men are from Mars, all righty," she said, signaling the waiter for more wine. "The question is, how do we get them to go back?" Straightening, she slapped the table with her palm. "Hey, a couple hundred torpedoes would do the trick."

Jessica giggled, and Gina shot her a second look. Women who looked like Jessica did not giggle. Which of course made Gina start giggling herself. Libby frowned until Gina nudged her shoulder and the blonde ended up joining them in a fit of bawdy laughter.

Normally Gina didn't drink all that much, and for some reason, wine and beer got to her quicker than anything else. She had to stop soon, or not only was she in for a whopper of a headache, but she wouldn't be able to form a coherent thought.

She squinted at the clock behind the bar but couldn't tell if the small hand was pointing to the five or the six. It didn't matter. No way was she going to be able to calculate what time zone she was actually operating in.

Standing in her way and misunderstanding what she was trying to do, their waiter winked at her. Glaring back, she lifted her empty glass to him. She wanted more wine. Not his unwelcome attention.

"I think," Jessica said, leaning forward over the round wooden table, "that we should make a pact. Right here. Right now."

The waiter arrived with a new bottle of wine and started refilling their glasses. Gina opened her mouth to give him an earful, but Libby, obviously sensing trouble, put a hand on her arm. Gina contented herself with a dirty look at that male-type person, then said, "Well? Let's hear about this pact."

Jessie stared earnestly into their eyes. "I say we swear off men for good."

Slowly Gina started to nod. She wasn't terribly sure about this, but Jessie looked so serious and maybe a little hurt, Gina didn't know what else to do.

Libby darted a nervous look at Gina. Then she nodded twice, stopped, and turned to Jessica. "For good, as in the rest of our lives?"

Jessica nodded, too. "Yep."

"I don't know about that," Gina said, finally deciding that concept was just too hard to swallow. "They can be pretty useful."

Jessie's lips thinned. "As far as I can tell, there's only one thing a man can do that's of any use at all."

"Yeah, but that one thing is a doozy," Gina said.

"What?" Libby asked, her forehead creasing. "What one thing?"

"We're modern women. There are ways to get around that," Jessie said, and then mumbled something about batteries.

Gina grinned.

Libby's blue eyes rounded. "Oh."

"Jessie, hon, I don't think the answer is to cut your-self off from men entirely." Gina took a sip while pon-dering the solution. "I think the trick is to know how to use them."

She paused, waiting for her new friends' responses. The flash of admiration she saw in Jessie's eyes prompted a fresh surge of shame and made Gina feel like a fraud. It was easy to sit here and be blasé after the fact. Hadn't she been just as sucked in by Nick? But of course, these women understood.

"Selectivity," Jessica said. "I can see your point."

"Right, reel 'em in, throw back the little ones, put the big ones to work, then move on."

Libby's eyes widened in confusion, and Jessie pro-ceeded to explain the concept to her. Gina just sipped her wine and thought about how different they all were, yet how close she suddenly felt to them, sitting here in a bistro in one of the most romantic cities in the world, getting sloshed.

Where the hell were all the good men? And when you did find one you thought could be *the one,* why did he have to end up being a jerk? Here they were, all reasonably attractive, intelligent women, so why did they attract losers? Maybe Jessie was right. Maybe swearing off men was the answer.

Gina snapped out of her reverie and impulsively reached across the table to wrap one hand around Jessie's and the other around Libby's. "Maybe you can beat the odds, Jessie. Maybe we all can."

"Maybe," Jessie said, without conviction. "But I'm not betting the farm on it."

"You know what?" Libby said, her voice unsteady.

Gina blinked and stared at the petite blonde. She'd bet this was the first time a guy had stood Libby up. During the past hour they'd found out a lot about each other. Naive, optimistic Libby was the Meg Ryan of Texas; cool, reserved Jessica the Grace Kelly of the West Coast, and Gina—well, she was just a mutt from Brooklyn.

"What?" Jessica asked.

"We're in Rome! And since we're here, I think we should go to the fountain."

"What fountain?" Gina asked.

"The Trevi Fountain. Like in that movie. *Three Coins in the Fountain*. You know, those three women were in Rome and they threw a coin into the fountain and made a wish? And Rossano Brazzi was in it, too."

Jessica's lips curved in a serene smile. Gina frowned as Libby went on with her explanation. Gina recalled the movie immediately. She wasn't sure she shared Libby's enthusiasm, but she shrugged and added, "There was that French guy, too. He was a count or something."

Libby turned to Jessie. "Didn't you see it?"

Jessie shrugged too. "Sure I did."

"Then what do you say?" Libby asked and signalled for the check.

Gina started rooting through her purse for some money. It wasn't like she had anything else to do now that the creep Nick had chumped her. Besides, the fountain wasn't far. She'd seen it from the cab on the way to the villa.

After they'd settled their bill and arranged to stash their luggage in the bistro's back room, they headed outside in the direction the waiter pointed them. It was late afternoon, and the sun, although still hot, was headed for the horizon.

The sidewalks were crowded with tourists and locals alike, the distinction between the two generally made by fresh loaves of bread sticking out of large mesh grocery bags for the night's dinner. Many strollers had already retired to the umbrella-shaded sidewalk cafés and sat behind mugs of beer while they people-watched. Most of them were couples. Holding hands. Whispering. And Gina got ticked off at Nick all over again.

"There." Libby pointed ahead of them, her voice rising in her excitement. "There it is. Wow! I had no idea it would be so big."

"Quite impressive, I have to admit," Jessie said, and hurried to keep up with Libby.

The tallest one of the three, Gina easily kept abreast of them as she scanned the area for another bistro with a view of the fountain. She was impressed, too. But she'd be more impressed if she was sitting down with a cup of coffee. Strong. Black. She squinted as the fuzziness in her head turned into an ache. The long walk and sun confirmed that she'd probably had one too many glasses of wine. Maybe even two.

"Excuse me, beautiful ladies."

The heavily accented voice came from behind Jessie, and when she moved to turn around, Gina saw that it belonged to a boy of about twelve.

"Are you speaking to us?" Jessie asked.

"Beautiful lady, of course," he said, his wide grin displaying several gaps in his teeth. "You are the most pretty ladies here."

Oh, bother. What did he want? Gina turned back to scoping out three empty seats as she listened to him offer to tell the legend of the Trevi Fountain for five thousand lira.

Excited, Libby started asking questions right away, but the boy clammed up and put out his hand.

Gina sighed. This could be a long afternoon. She swept another gaze to the left of the fountain, but there were no empty seats in sight. She turned back in time to see Libby handing over some lira. "Hey, kid, you'd better not run off," Gina said, crossing her arms over her chest.

Libby sent her a disapproving frown before blinking at the boy, her expression turning to one of mild suspicion as she let go of the money.

He took the bills and quickly stuffed them into his pocket. "I am Mario, a man of my word," he said. "This fountain is the most famous in all of Rome. There is a legend that, if one throws a coin into the fountain, then one must return to Italy and to Rome and this place. But I will tell you another legend...one that only some, such as myself, know for truth. This legend, it is very powerful magic. When the coin first touches the water of the Trevi, at that moment, if the heart makes a wish, it will come true. It cannot be otherwise. I tell you this because you are beautiful ladies and I wish for you that your special wish comes true."

"Is that right?" Jessie asked, a small smile tugging at her mouth.

"I tell you, lady, it's the truth. You throw your coin in now. You make a wish. It will come true."

Gina snorted. "I suppose it'll only work with silver dollars." What a great scam. The little sucker probably came back after dark and supplemented the ill-gotten lira by wading through the water.

Libby dove into her purse. "Come on. What do we have to lose?"

She withdrew a quarter and she closed her eyes, looking young and hopeful standing there near the edge of the water, and Gina and Jessie exchanged another glance. It wasn't too hard to guess what she would wish for. Of the three, Libby was definitely the least jaded. She'd find the right man. Probably have half a dozen kids and live happily ever after back in Texas.

Oh, what the hell. Gina shoved a hand into her purse pocket. She patted around until she felt the thin ridges of a dime, then she smiled and continued until she found a quarter.

She wouldn't close her eyes and make a wish, though. She was just doing this so Libby wouldn't get all upset. Gina took a deep breath, the coin poised atop her thumbnail.

Well, maybe one small wish wouldn't hurt. After all, she had three days in Rome to kill. And she was all the wiser now. She sucked in her lower lip, allowed her eyes to close ever so briefly, then leaned forward and sent the coin sailing through the air.

Libby's delighted laugh made her straighten, and she sent a sheepish look over her shoulder. From several feet away, a tall, good-looking man with dark hair smiled and nodded at her. With narrowed eyes, she glanced back at the fountain. She hadn't wished for another man. That would be stupid.

Of course, so was thinking of becoming a nun. The next time opportunity knocked in the form of a man, she'd have enough good sense to run the other way. That's all she wanted. Unless...

Sadly, she shook her head and gazed at the ripples her coin had made in the water. She'd been enough of a sap for one day.

"Your turn, Jessica," Libby said.

"I don't think so." Jessie had taken a step back.

"Come on," Gina prodded. "What's the worst that can happen?"

Jessie didn't budge. She simply stared at the fountain with a hesitant yet strange look on her face that Gina couldn't read.

"Don't be a chicken," Gina said, while Libby threw in a clucking noise. She wasn't sure if it was the incongruity of that sound coming from the petite blonde or the result of too much wine, but they all started giggling, and then Jessie started digging through her purse.

Gina dabbed at her eyes and at the same time swept her admirer a furtive glance. He'd gotten a little closer, and she lifted her chin with satisfaction. She wasn't interested, she was having fun with Libby and Jessie, but after the disaster with Nick, the attention was like a salve to her wounded ego.

Jessie flicked her coin into the air. As soon as it hit the water, their little Italian friend dramatically cleared his throat. They all turned to look at the boy.

"Ah," he said. "Now, sorrowfully, beautiful ladies, I must tell you that only one wish will be granted."

"What?" Libby's shoulders sagged. "Why?"

"What kind of scam are you running, you little twerp?" Gina demanded.

The boy started backing away. "I only tell the legend, lady. I don't make it up."

Gina shrugged. "Hey, you two fight over it. I didn't really make a wish."

Both women gave her bland, *yeah-right* looks, and she felt suitably sheepish. "Okay, maybe a little one."

Someone bumped her from behind. She turned and found her admirer alarmingly near. Refusing to return his smile, she stepped closer to Jessie. "I've seen enough of the fountain. How about you two?"

Libby nodded, casting one last longing look at the spray of water. "I'm going to try and get a flight back to Dallas tonight. Either one of you headed for the airport?"

Jessie pressed two fingers to her temple. "I haven't thought it through yet. I'll probably at least stay overnight."

Gina shook her head. "I have to pick up a package in Zurich in three days to take back to New York, so I figured I'd just hang around here."

No one spoke for a moment. It was strange to think they'd all just met hours ago. It felt like they'd been friends forever.

"Well, okay, I'd like your addresses and phone numbers," Libby finally said, and the sadness in her voice made Gina's insides go as soft as a toasted marshmallow as she scribbled the information into the small notebook Libby handed her.

"I'd like yours, too." Gina grinned. "If either of you ever get to New York, I'll take you for the best damn pizza you ever had."

While they finished exchanging addresses, Libby lay

claim to making the best apple pie west of the Mississippi, and Jessica's eyebrows drew together in an apologetic frown as she volunteered to show them the Getty Museum in Los Angeles.

Gina and Libby laughed, then allowed another brief but awkward silence to fall. They were all so different, yet they shared a common bond. It was hard saying goodbye.

"Well, I'd really better get moving," Libby said. "I think there's a flight available in a couple of hours, and I don't know how many choices I'll have after that."

"You'll have to get your things from the bistro. We can get a cab back with you, then you can go on to the airport from there," Jessie said, a smile returning to her lips.

"Great." Libby's big blue eyes lit up.

But they were still moist, and when Libby sniffed, Gina had to swallow back the threatening lump in her own throat. Without saying a word, she turned to flag a cab. She wasn't good at this goodbye stuff. She never, ever cried. As a kid, all tears had ever gotten her was ridiculed and humiliated. You did not want to be a soft touch in her tough Brooklyn neighborhood. Yet she felt suspiciously close to tears right now.

It was the wine, she figured, and Nick and jet lag and being so tired she'd need toothpicks for her eyes soon. She shook her head to clear the crippling fog of emotion. She had to stop this nonsense, figure out what to do next.

She must have started looking as bad as she felt because her erstwhile admirer had suddenly disappeared. She told herself that was a good thing as she placed two fingers in her mouth and let out a whistle that made the other two jump.

That got the chatty cab driver's attention from across the street, and he zipped his car between traffic to stop in front of them. Gina opened the back door, then stepped aside.

Libby gave her a funny look before getting in. Jessie hesitated and motioned for her to go next, but Gina shook her head. She ducked down so Libby could hear, too. "Would you guys mind if I sat this one out?" She gave a casual shrug. "I've got some phone calls to make, a wire to send and, um——"

She stopped, glancing from one to the other, their startled looks softening to expressions of understanding. She took a quick breath. "I'll call," she said, tapping the side of the small black taxi and stepping back to let Jessie in.

"I'll leave word at the bistro when I decide what I'm doing," Jessie whispered as she slid inside.

"Good." Gina straightened and hitched her purse up higher on her shoulder, hoping her hand would quit shaking. It didn't, so she kept it wrapped around the strap instead of lifting it in farewell. "Be safe, Libby," she called as the cab pulled away from the curb.

She sniffed, watching the taillights disappear, then reached into her purse for her compact. She found it easily. Too easily. Something wasn't right.

Her eyes widened at the blur of scattered makeup, empty gum wrappers and business cards, and she choked back the bitter taste of panic. Where the hell was her wallet?

Chapter Two

As Jackson Maxwell Covington III descended the staircase to the embassy's reception area, something told him today wasn't going to be like any other Monday. Being a practical man, he normally didn't pay attention to small inner voices except when it came to business, and arguably there was more to those types of feelings than something as nebulous as instinct.

But today was different. Today he sensed trouble. He'd tried to shake the eerie feeling during his usual breakfast of bran and orange juice, but it had persisted through his shaving ritual, which ended with a nick on his chin that had nearly caused him to bleed on his white shirt. That in itself would have been a disaster. The laundry had messed up again and had neglected to use enough starch. Which meant the shirts had been returned and he was inexplicably and annoyingly down to the one on his back.

Stopping midway down the stairs, he reached into his jacket pocket for his trusty leather-bound notepad. It had been a useful gift from his father, who himself had been a diplomat, as had been Jackson's grandfather.

He quickly jotted himself a note to remind housekeeping to dust the frames of the oil paintings on the wall next to the curved staircase. Tamping down his impatience over such blatant neglect, he slipped the notebook back into his jacket, adjusted his left cuff link and continued down the stairs.

The influx of hapless tourists had started earlier than usual today, he noted as he glanced toward the double entry doors. A family of four was lugging twice as many suitcases toward the receptionist. Behind them, three older ladies fanned themselves, talking in unison, their mouths moving faster than an Olympic judge's clock. Several other people milled around the lobby, and Jackson wondered why so many people appeared to be unescorted. Although, since they'd obviously made it past the *carabinieri,* he wasn't worried. The Italian police who guarded the embassy were all top-notch.

He was about to turn the corner when he saw her out of the corner of his eye. The crick he'd had in his neck for the past two days snapped free of tension as he swung back for a second look.

She would have been hard to miss. Already taller than anyone else in the lobby, she stood on tiptoes, try-ing to see past the crowd, her short denim skirt riding halfway up her tanned thighs. He noticed her toes, which peeked out from absurdly high-heeled, strappy black sandals. Her toenails were pink. So pink, in fact, he wouldn't doubt the polish had a name like Come and Get Me Pink.

Jackson's tie nearly choked him. He slipped a finger between the silk and his Adam's apple and loosened the knot. His skin was hot to the touch, and he frowned. Maybe he was coming down with something, a bug he might have picked up in Greece last week.

Maybe that was why he'd been having such odd sensations this morning.

Feeling foolish yet reassured, he glanced once more at the woman before continuing on his way, idly wondering if she were Italian or American. Her shiny dark brown hair nearly blended in with the mahogany curio cabinet behind her, disguising its length and style, but as she ducked down to adjust a sandal strap, he saw that it hung right below her jaw.

His gaze moved to her offending sandal...and her rising skirt. God help him, but if she bent down one more inch...

Jackson fumbled with the knot of his tie, stunned to realize that his heated reaction had nothing to do with a bug he might have picked up in Greece.

What the hell was wrong with him? Come and Get Me Pink was not his style. Sleek, sophisticated women were. He shook his head, smoothed down his tie and ignored the strange look a passing embassy guard gave him. Without giving the woman another glance, Jackson hurried toward the ambassador's office, wishing he could shake the annoying feeling of impending doom.

"WHAT DO YOU MEAN I have to wait? I've already been here for two hours." Gina drummed her fingers on the receptionist's desk. The embassy was getting more crowded by the minute, and she was starting to get warm and claustrophobic. She unfastened the top two buttons of her blouse. "How long does it take to get a new passport? Surely you can call New York and verify that I'm an American citizen."

The woman peered at Gina over heavy, black-framed glasses. Her keen, inflexible green eyes narrowed with irritation. She'd obviously been running interference at the embassy for a long time, and she was darn good at it. Few people could shut Gina up with a single look.

"Patience will go a long way toward getting you back on the right side of the law," the woman said, before nailing Gina with another four seconds of quiet disapproval.

Right side of the law? Gina quit drumming her fingers. "I'm the victim here. Someone stole *my* passport and *my* money."

Her outrage fell on deaf ears. Without so much as a glance in Gina's direction, the woman picked up the phone, punched in some numbers, spoke a few words, replaced the receiver, then turned her attention again to her computer terminal.

Gina glanced down at the nameplate on the desk. "Look, Ms. Morgan," she said, pasting a smile on her face. "I have to get to Switzerland by tomorrow evening. I have about three bucks and one suitcase. And I had to drag that sucker sixteen blocks to get here because I didn't have cab fare. I have no place to stay, and if I don't get something to eat soon I may pass out right across your desk. So I'm sure you understand why I'm just a teensy bit edgy."

The woman slowly swiveled toward her, and Gina's smile faltered. Wow, she was good. Ms. Morgan's bland expression slid to one of indifference as she peered once again over her glasses. "Would you like a doughnut and coffee?"

"All that sugar on an empty stomach will probably make me puke."

For the first time, the woman smiled, the gesture dry and lacking amusement. "How kind of you to share that with me." She turned back to her computer and pressed a key to change screens.

Sighing, Gina sank back in her chair. She was stretching the truth a bit. Since last night, when, in desperation, she had barged her way in on poor Jessie, she and Jessie had polished off half the box of Godiva chocolates Nick's maid had turned her stubborn nose up at. Considering all the wine they'd consumed earlier, it was no wonder neither woman had felt well this morning.

Gina had also borrowed a few dollars from Jessie, enough to call home for more money, but not enough for breakfast. She'd refused to take anything beyond that, no matter how much Jessie had urged her to do so. Gina hated feeling indebted, and she'd felt awful for having awoken Jessie in the middle of the night to beg a place to stay. Besides, her brother would wire her the money within the hour, and she'd be fine. She just hoped her bozo nephew had turned down his stereo long enough to get the message straight.

Gina plucked repeatedly at the collar of her blouse, trying to get some cool air circulating down between her very warm breasts. Either the embassy was being cheap with their air-conditioning, or her frazzled nerves were starting to take their toll.

"Ms. Morgan?" Gina began, and as much as it pained her, smiled and politely waited until the receptionist looked up. "I wouldn't lose my turn if I were to step outside, would I?"

The woman's impatient expression turned to one of concern as her gaze rested on Gina's face. "Are you all right?"

She shrugged. "Just a little warm."

Ms. Morgan clearly thought she was going to make good on her threat to puke or pass out, Gina realized. The woman angled away from her computer to study her, an anxious frown creasing her forehead. Gina pressed her lips together to keep them from curving in triumph. The woman's mistaken conclusion could speed things along, and Gina didn't want to blow the opportunity.

Hoping for subtlety, she took a deep, visible breath, then slumped slightly against the back of the chair, looking around distractedly, fanning herself.

She tried to keep track of Ms. Morgan out of the corner of her eye, but somehow the movement or angle disoriented her, and for a second, her vision blurred. A fist of nausea gripped her stomach, forcing her to swallow in panic.

"You don't look well," the woman said. "Are you sure you're all right?"

"What?" She turned, trying to focus, and swallowed again. "I—I'm fine."

This was great. Just great. She actually did feel slightly light-headed. It was nothing, she told herself, and straightened. This stunt reminded her of grade school, when, unprepared for algebra tests, she'd pretended she was ill. She'd ended up sicker than a dog every time. She figured she was getting punished for not studying. Either that, or her nerves had done her in for lying to the nuns.

"I think you'd better have a drink of water, or maybe even lie down. Your coloring doesn't look right." The previously unruffled Ms. Morgan's brows rose toward her reddish-blond hair as she leaned across her desk and touched Gina's arm. "You're awfully hot."

A nervous giggle rose in her throat. She'd wanted Nick to utter those words last night. But Nick was a rat. And she was here in Rome alone. She sniffed and pushed the hair away from her face. Her palms felt clammy. "I'll be fine."

"Oh, Mr. Covington." Ms. Morgan's gaze skittered toward a tall, dark-haired man in a navy blue suit who was passing behind the etched glass divider that isolated the reception desk.

He slowed, his irritation at being waylaid obvious by the frown he swung in their direction. His eyes briefly met Gina's, and they were such a startlingly bright shade of blue that her pulse jerked.

"Mr. Covington," Ms. Morgan continued, "I'm very sorry to bother you, but I'm afraid this young lady may need to go somewhere and lie down, and I can't leave the desk."

"No, I don't." Gina gripped the arms of the chair. Those blue eyes were on her again, but she was having trouble focusing on them. She dropped her gaze to his unimaginative maroon tie. That didn't help. She blinked, but her vision remained slightly blurred.

A hand was suddenly in front of her, a large hand, palm out. "Here, let me help you."

His voice was low and slightly raspy and had no business belonging to that awful Brooks Brothers tie. She glanced up...to those incredible eyes.

"I can get up by myself," she said, then when the room swayed, she quickly slipped her hand in his, afraid she'd embarrass herself by passing out across the desk with her butt sticking up in the air. "Where are we going?"

He frowned in silence for a moment. "My office."

"What about my suitcase?"

"I'll take care of it."

His grip was firm and sure as he helped her to her feet. She teetered backward, but he held her steady. When Gina looked up at him, his blue gaze intersected with hers and she got another funny feeling in the pit of her stomach.

"You'll be fine," he said in a deep, soothing voice, and for no reason, she believed him. He wouldn't let her make a fool of herself in the middle of this stuffy lobby. She knew this to be true. She didn't know how, she just did.

The entire notion was ridiculous. She didn't know him. Her feelings probably had more to do with having little choice but to accept his help. But when he offered her his other arm, she clung to it while he guided her around the desk.

Ms. Morgan stood suddenly, as if she were afraid she might have to catch her unwelcome ward. The receptionist was tall, nearly as tall as Gina. Few women hit the five-ten mark, and that alone upped her a notch in Gina's book.

She gave Ms. Morgan a weak grin. "Thanks. Uh, this doesn't mean I'll lose my place in line, does it?"

The older woman blinked, then a startled laugh escaped her pale pink lips. "No, Ms. Hart, I assure you we'll keep your paperwork going." Her gaze flickered to the man and lingered, her sandy eyebrows drawing together in a puzzled frown. "Thank you, Mr. Covington. I'll have some tea sent to your office."

"Never mind, Greta, I'll take care of it." He squeezed Gina's hand, ever so slightly before loosening his hold, as though the gesture was impulsive and promptly regretted. "My office is on the second floor," he said, looking down into her eyes, his gaze holding hers captive. "Will you be able to manage the stairs?"

"Sure," Gina said, finally looking away when the

intensity of his stare started to make the back of her neck tingle. Her gaze collided with Greta's speculative one. The woman had not yet resumed her seat. She stood, in her impeccably tailored taupe suit and white silk blouse, eyeing them with furtive interest, her attention drawing from their still-joined hands to their bowed faces.

Greta Morgan was in love with Mr. Covington.

Gina blinked, wondering why the idea had popped into her head. All she cared about was having some place to sit down until the dizziness passed.

She dropped her hand from his. "You know, I think I'm feeling better already." She swayed, and his arm slipped around her waist.

"Greta, maybe you'd better order that tea. And perhaps a light snack." He started to lead Gina away, and feeling a little too weak to protest, she threw the other woman a helpless look.

The receptionist smiled, her perfectly manicured fingers already reaching for the phone. "You'll be fine," she assured Gina. "You're in the best of hands."

She didn't look upset after all, and Gina admired her composure. And then it hit her. Of course the woman wasn't upset. She was attractive, obviously cultured and as classy as they came. Why should she consider Gina a threat?

Her stomach cramped, and she fought the reflexive desire to hang on to her escort. He was close, one arm still hooked protectively around her, the silky fabric of his expensive suit whispering against her cheek. The faint scent of something spicy and male momentarily interfered with her balance.

If nothing else came of this lousy trip, Gina figured she had learned one lesson. God, but she hated to admit that her rowdy, pain-in-the-neck brothers were right. But from now on, she was sticking to her own kind.

AS SOON AS THEY ENTERED his office, Jackson headed for the windows and slanted the miniblinds to dilute the bright early-afternoon sun that was throwing blinding light across his off-white, raw silk sofa. When he turned back to the woman, she was looking around his office with a wrinkled nose.

His gaze was automatically drawn to the most recent object of her attention, a trio of original oil paintings hanging on the wall behind his massive mahogany desk—the same paintings that had once hung behind his father's desk and his father's before him.

"Take the sofa," he said, and grabbed the crystal decanter of water sitting on a silver tray to the right of his credenza. "Feel free to lie down and put your feet up."

She gave him a funny look, peered down at the couch, then glanced back at him with a wary expression. "Really?"

He frowned. What did she think he meant? His attention spanned the exposed length of tanned legs, the Come and Get Me Pink-tipped toes....

He cleared his throat, reached for a Waterford crystal tumbler and poured the water. "I thought you might be more comfortable."

She swung a leg up, bending it at the knee to inspect the bottom of her sandals. "I don't want to screw up your couch."

He had to briefly look away. Normally, a pair of legs didn't set him off like this, but a sudden flash of heat was sending his concentration out the window. Maybe because hers were bare and long and...

She sat on the edge of the sofa, her skirt riding as high as it possibly could without waving the flag, and she slipped off her sandals. "Sorry to be so much trouble," she said, starting to cross her legs. "I'm sure you're busy and—"

She stopped short and stared at him in open surprise as he gulped down the water he'd poured.

He blinked at the sudden silence. Realizing what he'd done, he quickly discarded the empty tumbler, grabbed another, filled it and passed it to her.

"Thanks." She sipped while watching him over the rim of her glass. "I'm feeling better already. It was stuffy downstairs, but it's nice and cool up here."

She plucked at the open collar of her shirt, and he got a straight shot of deep, inviting cleavage. An unexpected current of desire bolted through him. He backed up, straightening his tie. This was ridiculous. He was thirty-seven, not some randy teenager. Besides, he didn't even know this woman.

"By the way, I'm Jackson Covington," he said as he rounded his desk, putting the massive piece of mahogany between them. "I'm an assistant to the consul general."

"I'm Gina Hart," she said distractedly, and he felt his face crease into a frown. "This is the embassy, right?"

She looked a little dazed again, but she was obviously lucid enough to understand the difference between an embassy and a consulate. "You're in Rome, at the embassy," he assured her as he seated himself. "I work for the consulate, but I'm here on special assignment." One that would put him on the fast track to a consul general's position. He hoped.

She nodded absently, her gaze wandering to the nameplate on his desk, and the confusion disappeared. Eyes sparkling, she said, "Jackson Maxwell Covington, *the third,* huh?"

A hint of a smile lifted one corner of her mouth and made her eyes an appealing shade of brown. She took another sip of water, her eyes staying fastened to his, and he wondered if she knew what she was doing to him. As much as he tried to ignore the sensation, his body hummed with the uncomfortable realization that he was highly and inexplicably attracted to this woman.

Fortunately, he didn't think she was aware of his reaction. She'd certainly done nothing overtly to encourage it. In fact, she still looked pale, and her hand was unsteady as she continued to slowly sip from the tumbler. Which made him feel like a heel. He was supposed to be rescuing her, not lusting after her.

The whole idea of lusting after anyone sent another wave of surprise over him. He straightened abruptly and glanced at the eighteen-karat gold-trimmed silver nameplate. The one Miranda had given him for his birthday three years ago.

At the thought of Miranda, guilt seeped into his conscience. He promptly banished it. They weren't engaged, weren't even close, no matter what everyone expected.

"That's right," he said finally. "My full name is Jackson Maxwell Covington III."

"So, what does everyone call you? Jack? Max?"

"Jackson." He lifted a brow. "Or Mr. Covington."

"Oh, I guess that was my cue." She shrugged one shoulder. "You can call me Gina. My middle name is Marie, but I don't use it. Unless I'm getting arrested or something."

Nonplused, he stared at the serious look on her face, then caught the mischievous twinkle in her eye before she glanced away to gaze out the window.

"I'm glad to see you're feeling better, Ms. Hart," he said, leaning back in his chair to study her further. "How did you come to be here at the embassy?"

"My passport and money got ripped off."

"Where?"

"At the Trevi Fountain."

"I see." He smiled. Due to the success of a popular old movie, American tourists loved the Trevi Fountain, and the Italians loved the small fortune in coins they left behind.

"You see?" She set down the glass, her eyebrows drawing together in a combative expression. "If you think I went there to make some sappy wish, you're wrong."

He frowned as she tried to push to her feet. "Lots of tourists go there to make a wish."

"Not me." She sank back into the sofa as though the effort to stand had been too much.

"When did this happen?" he asked, glancing at his watch and wondering where the devil the tea and snack were that Greta had ordered.

"Yesterday."

"Money, credit cards, everything is gone?"

"The slime bucket didn't even leave me enough for cab fare." She picked up a coaster and used it to fan herself.

"Are you here alone?" he asked while reaching for the phone and pressing an extension.

She shook her head as though admonishing herself, a brief, humorless laugh breaching her lips. "Yeah."

He held up a finger to her when someone in the kitchen answered, but he noticed that she was staring out the window, lost in thought.

"This is Jackson Covington," he said, speaking into the phone but keeping his eyes on her. "I have a tray coming to my office. Would you make sure you include some cool, damp towels, some chilled juice and something with sugar, maybe a couple of cookies?"

Abruptly, she turned to meet his gaze and mouthed something.

A smile tugged at the corners of his mouth. "Make that anything chocolate."

She grinned and gave him a thumbs-up sign.

"And I'd like that delivered right away, please." His request acknowledged, he hung up. "Where did you spend last night?" he asked, looking back at her.

"In a hotel with a friend. Someone I met yesterday."

His eyes narrowed at the odd expression on her face, at the way she hedged, as if this was a subject she'd rather avoid. Then her chin lifted, and he knew she thought he was being judgmental. Which he probably was, because it irrationally bothered him that she'd spent the night with someone she just met.

"A woman," she added, and stopped fanning herself. "Not that it's any of your business."

He nodded his head in agreement. "You're right."

"Don't give me that look. She isn't *that* kind of friend."

He stared, confused for a moment, then laughed. "The thought hadn't occurred to me."

A sly, devilish grin curved her lips. "Why? Does the idea offend your sensibilities?"

"I thought you were feeling ill," he said blandly.

"You should see me when I'm up to par." She gave a shaky laugh, then her lips flattened. "It's getting hot in here."

He rose and turned to the credenza for more water. When she passed him her glass for a refill, her fingers felt warm. He hesitated after pouring the water.

"Do you think it might be more than heat or exhaustion? You could be coming down with something."

She grabbed for the drink like a beggar eager for a scrap of bread. "I don't think so. I don't get sick often."

He didn't move, and after she took a large gulp of water, she slowly raised her gaze to his. "What?" she asked, a guarded look narrowing her eyes.

Jackson lifted a palm within inches of her forehead. "May I?"

"What are you, a part-time nurse?" she said, but pushed her face slightly forward, indicating her permission to be touched.

He brushed her bangs aside. Her hair was even softer than it looked. "You're burning up," he said, his palm pressed to her skin.

She sighed and sat back, breaking contact. "I already told you that, Jack."

"I'm going to call a doctor," he said, ignoring the hideous nickname she used.

"No, you are not." She straightened again. "I don't want any doctor poking me. I'm serious. I'll leave before he gets here."

He'd known her for less than half an hour, but he didn't doubt her stubborn threat. "We have to do something for you."

"Well, there is one thing that would help."

"Name it."

She blew out a stream of air that stirred her bangs. When she plucked at her collar again he stepped back so he wouldn't have such a bird's-eye view down the front of her shirt.

"If you wouldn't mind," she said, "I'd be much cooler with my blouse off."

Chapter Three

Her fingers reached for a button, and Jackson edged backward until the desk hit the back of his legs and the corner of his in-box poked his butt.

"Stop," he said, putting up a warning hand. Perspiration coated his nape. His palms itched with sudden clamminess. "You can't do that."

She raised perplexed eyes, her fingers stilling. Then she smiled. "Oh, don't worry, Jack. I have a sports bra underneath. It's okay."

"Don't call me Jack. And for God's sake, don't take that blouse off." Someone knocked at the door. He inhaled sharply and started to move. "In fact, don't do anything. Just sit there. Got it?"

"Women exercise in sports bras all the time. Don't you see them running in the park?"

He paused with his hand on the doorknob and sent her a scathing look.

"Okay, okay." She dropped her hand to her lap and gave him an exasperated look. "I'll just sit here and die of the heat. But make sure you send my body back to New York. My address is on my luggage."

He waited another second, hoarding his composure,

before opening the door slowly, leaving it only slightly ajar.

"Good afternoon, Mr. Covington. I have your—"

"Fine, Roberto." Jackson blocked the waiter's passage, then ignored the man's startled reaction. "I'll take this."

Forced to open the door wider in order to accept the tray, he noticed the curious look the waiter darted over Jackson's shoulder. Unable to resist, he glanced back to see what Roberto saw. Gina was lounging back on the sofa, her long, bare legs stretched out in front of her, and she wiggled her fingers in greeting. The other man smiled back.

"She lost her passport," Jackson said, the explanation sounding lame and totally unnecessary. "And she's feeling unwell."

Roberto nodded and smiled. It was a smug, knowing smile, an irritating one.

Jackson did not return it. He wasn't going to wait for the heat or a fever to do it. He was going to kill Gina Hart himself.

"Thank you, Roberto," he said in a stern voice, and the man swiftly got the hint and turned away.

He closed the door with the toe of his custom-made Italian loafer and brought the tray into the room. He made a point of not looking at her as he set the tea on the glass coffee table.

"Mr. Covington," she began with emphasis, "I don't know what your filthy little mind thought I was suggesting, but it's hotter than hell in here and this heavy cotton blouse is not helping matters."

He looked up then and caught the challenging lift of her chin. "My filthy little mind simply does not consider it proper for you to disrobe in my office."

She held his gaze. "Don't worry. Your virtue is safe. I don't go for uptight prigs." She leaned back in a show of nonchalance, but he saw that the fevered dampness around her jaw was causing her hair to cling to her skin, and her lips had grown pale. "Bet you didn't think I knew that word."

"You should try to eat something." He unwrapped the little finger sandwiches and passed them to her. For all her bravado, she really didn't look well.

Suspicion puckered her brows. "What's that?"

He peered closer. "These are cucumber." He swiveled the plate around. "And these others are filled with cream cheese and black olives."

"Oh, yummy." She rolled her eyes and let her head fall back against the sofa. "Anyway, I'm hot, not hungry."

He rammed a hand through his hair. Ms. Hart was becoming more trouble than he'd bargained for. "I'm calling a doctor."

"No, please." She sat up straight, her hand shooting out to wrap around his forearm. Her eyes were wide with uncertainty and maybe a little fear, and her sudden display of vulnerability made his irritation dissolve. "I really, really hate doctors."

He set aside the sandwiches. "We may not have a choice," he said, picking up one of the rolled white terry towels. When she opened her mouth to protest, he lifted a silencing hand. "But for now, we'll see if we can get the fever down."

She nodded and released his arm. Gently, with a light touch at her shoulder, he urged her to lie back. She put out a hand for the towel, but he brushed aside her bangs and laid the cool cloth across her forehead himself.

"Nice bedside manner, Jack," she said with a weak

smile, her eyes drifting closed, her limp hand sliding to rest an inch from his thigh. "I don't need a doctor. I have you."

The teasing words startled him, made him pensive. No one ever needed Jackson. Not personally, anyway. Not even Miranda. They had similar backgrounds and were well suited, a perfect match, most people thought, but did she *need* him?

He gazed down at Gina, who looked half asleep with her thick black lashes lying across her pale cheeks. Before he knew what he was doing, he'd trailed the pad of his thumb down her petal-soft skin. He laughed silently at himself. He doubted this woman needed him, either, but hearing her teasing words had unexpectedly tackled him at the knees.

She stirred, and he snatched his hand back the second before she opened her eyes to bare slits. "Hey, Jack, I could use another sip of water."

"How about some lukewarm tea?"

She shivered. "You lost me with the warm description. Water would be good."

He'd already made it to his credenza for the crystal carafe of Evian. "It seems to me people always drink tea when they're ill."

"It's psychological. Besides, I told you. I'm not ill. I'm hot."

And stubborn, but he prudently kept that thought to himself. "Here," he said, and when she started to sit up, he stilled her, slipping his free hand around her nape to support her while his other pushed the glass to her lips.

She took a long, slow drink, then slanted him a curious look. "Be careful. I could get used to this."

"You don't like uptight prigs, remember?"

Gina blushed. "They make good doctors, though."

"Do you always get in the last word?" He offered her another sip.

"I try." She drank deeply, then waved the glass away. "With seven brothers and sisters, I don't always win."

He released her when she tried to lie back again. Crouching down to accommodate her had put him in too intimate a position, so he quickly stood. "You were starting to drift off. Why don't you see if you can get some sleep?"

"Here?"

He shrugged. "It's quiet. I have some paperwork to do—"

She lifted on one elbow. "Hey, I'd better shove off and quit disturbing you—"

Jackson stopped her. "Sleeping, you won't disturb me. Now, talking is another matter...."

She stared in obvious surprise, and then her lips began to curve. "Well, well, Jack, there's hope for you yet."

"I'm relieved you think so. Either eat one of those sandwiches or close your eyes."

She made a face, then her expression perked up. "Hey, what happened to the chocolate?"

"There's a couple of truffles here, but I'm not sure that's a good idea. They're probably too rich."

Gina sighed. "Ah, Jack, you have so much to learn about me."

She smiled at him, one pale cheek starting to dimple as she snuggled down to get comfortable, her body curling toward him, and the suggestion of getting to know her jolted him with its sudden and surprising appeal. Of course, it wasn't possible.

"Pleasant dreams, Ms. Hart."

"I'm not really going to sleep. Just shutting my eyes for a minute," she said, her lashes already lowering. She pushed absently at the collar of her blouse, and with the top two buttons undone, the front of the fabric formed a deep V.

Taking a steadying breath, he looked away. She was right. It *was* getting rather warm in here.

He moved quietly around his desk and angled his appointment calendar toward him. He had a full afternoon of meetings, including a four o'clock with the chief of police that would inevitably lead to cocktails at La Rosetta.

He shook his head even as he reached for his phone, knowing what he was about to do was a mistake. His secretary answered on the first ring, and as he kept his gaze fastened on his peacefully slumbering guest, he instructed his longtime assistant to cancel his next appointment and reschedule his meeting with the police chief.

It wasn't difficult to interpret Marcy's brief pause before she acknowledged his request. Nothing short of death ever made him waver from his schedule. Without explanation, he thanked her and severed the phone connection. Before he could ring Greta, someone knocked at the door.

His gaze flew from the phone to Gina. Although she appeared somewhat restless, twisting a little and tugging at her skirt hem, her eyes remained closed and her sleep appeared to remain ultimately undisturbed.

Quickly he headed toward the door instead of calling out. He opened it and met Greta's anxious frown.

"How's our patient?" she asked in her usual brisk, no-nonsense tone.

"Sleeping." He stepped into the hall, closed the door behind him and managed to maintain a bland expression when all he could think about was how damn proprietary he'd just sounded.

Greta's surprise was clear in the widening of her green eyes. When she suddenly narrowed them, suspicious curiosity took over.

"I don't want to disturb her," he said, the need to offer the explanation about as welcome as the unusual heat wave they were having. "Is her paperwork finished?"

At his brusque tone, Greta's lips slowly curved. She was one of the few people around the embassy he couldn't rattle. They'd known each other too long.

"Uh, not yet," she said, frowning slightly at him, then turning to stare at the closed door. "We were swamped, and I figured she wasn't in any condition to go anywhere yet."

Her forehead creased the way it did when something puzzled her, and Jackson didn't miss the nervous way she fiddled with her antique silver brooch. Something was definitely up.

He glanced down at the papers she held in her other hand, and she quickly abandoned the brooch to roll them up, preventing him from seeing their contents.

"I was just on my way to Mr. Wellington's office with these contracts, and I thought I'd stop by to see how Ms. Hart was doing," she said, her chin lifting at a slight angle as if daring him to challenge her.

He gestured expansively toward the door. "You can see for yourself if you want."

Amusement arched one of her brows. "That's not necessary. I trust you're taking very good care of her."

There was no suggestion in her voice, but something

about the look she flicked him made him clench his jaw. What in the hell did Greta think was going on? Surely, she didn't think…

He fingered his tie. She knew him better than that. "Look, since you're going to Ray's office, anyway, mind taking something over for me?" he asked.

"Of course not."

He reached for the doorknob. Now she could see everything was just fine. Although he failed to understand how she could think anything else.

After opening the door, he stepped aside to let Greta precede him. She glided past him, then froze, blocking his entrance.

"Sorry," he said when he nearly collided with her.

She didn't seem to hear him or acknowledge that he'd almost run her down. Her attention was absorbed elsewhere. He followed her stare.

Gina lay sprawled out, still asleep, minus her shirt. Two soft-looking mounds of enticing flesh were barely contained by gray stretchy material. Twin pebbly peaks pushed at the fabric.

"What the devil—?" Jackson turned to meet Greta's startled eyes. He exhaled sharply. "She wasn't like that when I—"

"Do you have those papers for Mr. Wellington?" the receptionist interrupted calmly, an unreadable expression replacing her surprise.

He nodded, a stunned fog clouding his brain as he continued toward his desk, making a conscious effort not to glance Gina's way. Stopping suddenly, he faced Greta. "She's been complaining about the heat. She must have removed her shirt in her sleep."

"Sounds reasonable," she said, shrugging one shoulder, then inclining her head toward his desk. "The papers?"

Her obtuseness sparked his anger. And then he realized Greta was just being Greta. She was always calm and efficient and reasonable, never one to overreact. He was the one who was ready to pop an artery over this absurd situation.

"Look, Greta, you're going to have to do something else with her. She can't lie around here dressed like this...." He pushed a hand through his hair. "She can't stay here, period."

"Oh, for heaven's sake, Jackson, three minutes ago you were worried about disturbing her." She grabbed the papers he'd picked up off his desk. "Take an early walk around Villa Borghese tomorrow morning. You won't see the women joggers wearing anything different. In fact, getting away from your office for a change would do you some good."

That was the trouble with knowing someone too well. They felt at liberty to take jabs at you. He wasn't a workaholic, damn it. He *liked* his work. "How much sooner before her new passport is ready?" he asked. "An hour or two?"

"I doubt it. And then there's the issue of money. She's waiting for funds to be wired from New York."

"I'll pay her replacement costs."

Gina muttered something incoherent. Greta glanced over at her. Reluctantly, Jackson followed his friend's gaze.

Gina stretched in her sleep, one arm slowly, languidly rising at an angle above her head. Her legs were too long, her breasts too round and enticing. He had to get her out of here.

When he looked back to Greta for help, she was staring intently at him. "And then what?" she asked, her tone still calm and reasonable and inexplicably irritating. "We kick her out in the street until she gets some funds from her family? *If* she gets the funds from her family?"

"What do you usually do in a situation like this?"

She smirked on her way to the door. "Impose on friends. I'll check with you in another hour."

"Wait a minute."

"Hi, Ms. Morgan."

They both turned at the sound of Gina's husky, sleep-filled voice. She rubbed at one eye and squinted through the other. "Is my paperwork all set?"

"I'm still working on it," Greta said, her usual reserve giving way to a friendly smile. "Feeling any better?"

Jackson frowned. This was one hell of a day, all right. Gina Hart was even charming the unflappable Greta.

"Oh, I'll live." Gina struggled to raise herself.

"No need to get up," Greta said quickly.

He reared back his head. "Why not?"

Greta's disapproving gaze met his disbelieving one. "I have to get these papers taken care of. I'll let you know when Ms. Hart's passport is ready."

"I'm sure we can find someplace else for her to wait," he said, following her to the door.

"He's right," Gina said, but sent him a peevish look when he glanced at her. She was half sitting, half reclining, her left breast bunching and overflowing the stretchy bra as she leaned toward them. His heart skittered, and he abruptly turned away as she added, "I already told him I don't want to be in his way."

"Nonsense." Greta waved off the protest. "He's already canceled some of his appointments."

Jackson glared at her. They were going to have words…right before he strangled his big-mouthed secretary.

Gina started to say something else, but Greta reached for the doorknob and muttered something about ringing them later before she disappeared with a finite click.

Taking a deep breath, he stared at the closed door, bracing himself to face Gina. She was just another tourist. He met hundreds of them in the course of a month. And it *was* his job to assist them. No need to overreact.

He turned to find her staring down at her chest.

Slowly she raised puzzled eyes and asked, "Did you take my shirt off?"

He snorted. "No." The denial came out a sharp bark as he hurried around his desk and sank into the nebulous safety of his chair. "You did that in your sleep. Feel free to put it back on."

A stack of file folders sat in the corner of his desk, and he promptly plopped them in front of himself, preparing to dig into his work.

"You don't have to get testy," she said. "I have no intention of staying and bothering you any longer."

Jackson continued to stare down at the papers in front of him and picked up a pen. From his peripheral vision he caught her short, jerky movements and struggled against glancing up for a look. She was probably putting her blouse back on, and he'd be better off keeping his eyes right where they were.

He looked up.

One of her arms was already covered by a sleeve. Twisting her body, she pushed her other arm into the fabric, her breasts thrusting out in the process.

Her gaze connected with his. "Happy?" she asked, her brows arching. She adjusted her collar, then, making no move to button up, sank back against the sofa cushions and started fanning herself. Her pallor had turned to a dull pink flush. Probably due to fever. "Just give me a couple more minutes, then I'll be out of your hair."

He threw down his pen and exhaled sharply. "You're not going anywhere."

"Wanna bet?"

"Okay," he said slowly. "Where do you plan on going?"

She blinked, the defiance starting to fade from her eyes. "To the lobby to wait for my new passport."

"And you have money to pay for this?"

Her gaze flew to her watch, and her expression crumpled like a paper bag. "Oh, no. The wire office is closed for afternoon siesta, isn't it?"

"Yes. But they'll reopen in another hour."

She started fanning herself again, this time more briskly as she thoughtfully chewed at her lower lip and let her gaze wander idly out the window as if trying to formulate a plan.

"Look, I've turned the air down, but I'm thinking you should see a doctor. How about if I—"

"We've already gone through this, Jack. No doctor. Besides, I've had minor heat exhaustion before. It's no big deal."

"This might be something more serious."

"Well if it is, it isn't your problem. I'm going downstairs to sit with Ms. Morgan until the telegraph office opens."

"No, you're not. It's too warm and crowded down there." He stood when she pushed to the edge of the sofa and started buttoning her blouse. "I thought that sports bra thing was perfectly acceptable attire," he said dryly. "Why are you suddenly buttoning up to leave my office?"

She lifted her head, her eyes narrowing briefly before she grinned. "I'm just trying to protect your virtue, Jack. You almost had a conniption when that waiter came in, and I had all my clothes *on* then."

He started to deny her claim, then figured he was better off keeping his mouth shut. Let her go, he thought. He had too many other things to do to play nursemaid.

They lapsed into several moments of silence as she finished buttoning her blouse and gathering her things. He watched her take another long, slow sip of water, then shove the hair away from her face before standing. She teetered back, looking a little unsteady at first, her expression uncertain. Then her breasts rose and fell with the deep breath she took and she flashed him a brave smile.

Oh, hell. He scrubbed at his tired eyes. "Sit down. You're not going anywhere."

Her smile promptly disappeared and was replaced with a scowl. "Don't think I'm not grateful for your hospitality," she said, and started for the door, "but buzz off."

"Pardon me?"

She slowed but didn't stop. "You sound like my father, and even he quit trying to order me around five years ago."

"Gina."

It wasn't so much the plea he heard in his own voice that took him aback as it was the familiar use of her name. Clearly, he'd surprised her, too, because she stopped, turned and stared.

She blinked, one side of her mouth starting to curve. "Oh, Jack, I like the way you said that."

His tie felt snug. He adjusted the knot. "Uh, Ms. Hart, let's talk about this, uh, passport business."

Her smile faded and she looked disappointed. She opened her mouth to say something, then closed it again and shook her head.

The phone rang.

Jackson ignored it. "Greta should be done in short order. There's no reason for you to run off and—"

The phone rang again.

Eyeing it, Gina lifted her hand to the doorknob.

"You still haven't had anything to eat," he reminded her.

"You'd better get the phone."

It rang again. "My secretary will get it."

"Maybe it's Greta."

She had a point. He jerked the receiver to his mouth. "Covington."

The ambassador's assistant identified herself, then said, "Please hold for Ambassador Swanson."

Gritting his teeth, Jackson glanced at the ceiling. He couldn't very well ignore the ambassador. He adjusted the phone against his shoulder, reached for his pen, then motioned to Gina that he should only be a moment.

She was already gone.

Chapter Four

"What a moron," Gina muttered to herself.

Behind the counter, the woman's plump face creased in a frown and her tired-looking brown eyes darkened in warning. "Excuse me, *signorina?*"

"Oh, not you." Gina straightened, pushed herself away from the steadying comfort of the telegraph office's tiled counter and offered a sheepish grin. The last thing she could afford to do was alienate this woman.

"I was referring to my brother," Gina explained. "He was the one who was supposed to send me money."

The woman nodded, her indifference clear. "A *prossimo,*" she said. Angling sideways to view the long line that had formed behind Gina, she added, "Next," in lightly accented Italian.

"Wait a minute." Gina grabbed onto the counter. "I'm going to have to make another call."

"There is a telephone for the public around the corner."

"You wouldn't happen to have…I'd be calling collect." Gina smiled, wishing the clerk was a man. The woman peered back, unsmiling, obviously not impressed with Gina's charms or sympathetic to her predicament.

"I'm going to have to stand in line all over again, aren't I?" Gina asked, her knees beginning to feel a little weak again.

The woman nodded. "Next."

The people behind Gina started muttering angry remarks and she had little choice but to step aside.

At the same time she started to move away, a troubling thought occurred to her and she quickly shouldered herself back into position. "Excuse me," she said with an apologetic smile. "Just one more small thing," she told the clerk. "You wouldn't have a few lira to lend me?"

The woman's eyes grew larger than two supreme pizzas.

"I didn't think so." Gina sighed and stepped to the side once more, her pride as battered as the crumpled clothes she wore.

She was hot again and feeling a bit nauseous. The hike from the embassy to the telegraph office was longer than she'd remembered, and although it was already late afternoon and she hadn't had to battle the blistering midday sun, she had yet to recover from her first outing.

And now her brother, possibly the world's biggest nitwit, had left her stranded. Scratch that. She was the world's biggest nitwit for having relied upon him.

Slowly, she made her way toward the end of the counter, each leaden step a chore. To be fair, David wasn't really a jerk. A little absentminded, maybe, but of all her siblings, she could count on him the most. Besides, she'd receive the least amount of ridicule from him. He seemed to understand her better than the rest of the family. Even if he didn't agree with her need for independence or for a different sort of life than their Brooklyn neighborhood had to offer, at least he respected her right to make her own decisions.

"Pssst."

Gina stopped as she tried to identify the source of the sound behind her.

"Pssst. *Signorina?*"

Slowly she turned. Several feet away, a short, swarthy man grinned. A gold tooth caught the bright overhead light and gleamed.

"You talking to me?" Gina asked, getting a creepy-crawly feeling when the man let his gaze wander down to her legs. She shifted, putting more distance between them.

"*Si.*" He nodded, and his eyes lingered on her breasts before meeting her gaze. "You are in need of some lira?"

Gina laughed. "Not *that* bad, pal."

He shot her a quizzical look. "I can help you."

"Right." Resisting the urge to shiver, she glanced with reassurance at the crowd of people waiting in line before she turned and continued toward the phone.

"Wait, *signorina.*"

If she ignored him, the little twerp would eventually go away. She didn't need him hanging around when she made her call. She preferred to do her begging in peace.

She sighed. Besides, she was keeping her nose clean. The last thing she needed was another run-in with old Jack from the embassy. The sudden and unexpected image of Jackson Maxwell Covington's watchful blue eyes stopped her cold.

"Ah, good, *signorina,* you will listen." Mistaking her hesitation, the little man hurried around to face her.

She glared down at him. "Beat it."

He frowned, confusion making dark slashes of his brows. "I am here to help you."

"Want me to call the *policia,* the *carabinieri?*"

At the mention of the authorities, he swept a nervous glance to his right. When his gaze returned to hers, he smiled again, displaying the annoying gold tooth. "That is not necessary. I want only to offer you some help." He shrugged narrow shoulders. "But if you do not need my services..."

"Bingo." She hurried around him, leaving him looking puzzled and irritated.

Her reflexive desire to flee speeded her movements, and she was relieved to find the public phone available when she rounded the corner. Ten minutes and five answering machines later, her relief was replaced with apprehension.

Mentally, she ticked off her list of options. Her parents were on vacation in Florida, the twins were away at camp and her younger brother Buddy didn't have a phone. She'd even stooped to trying her big-mouthed older sister and risked an hour lecture, but no one was home. This was not good.

Of course, there was the embassy.

The idea of asking Jack for help again sent another shiver through her. He was an odd man. Not particularly her type, far too conservative and formal, yet with his unvarnished bedside manner, he'd unnerved her to the point that she'd foolishly fled the embassy without thinking things through.

Sure, she still needed to get her hands on some money. She doubted the embassy could do anything about her deadbeat brother, but she still wasn't feeling entirely well, and coming back out in the heat hadn't been her wisest course of action. She'd had bouts of heatstroke before, especially when she was sleep-deprived. A slight hangover didn't help. Rest, cool air and lots of water were the antidotes. Not running around like a crazy person, all because some guy made her edgy.

Shaking her head, she dug into her pocket for her last few coins, which she'd been saving for a cold drink, and deposited them into the phone slot. Why had she let herself get so worked up? She didn't even know Jack. Besides, what she did know of him reminded her of the type of man she had only yesterday promised herself she'd sworn off forever.

He was confident, powerful, polished, presumably rich and, okay, attractive, even if he did seem uptight. All and all, he reminded her that she was from Brooklyn and that she always had to stop and think about which piece of silverware to pick up every time there was more than a spoon or fork beside her plate.

And he reminded her that she'd come halfway across the world to make a complete fool of herself.

She finished dialing the hotel number and prayed Jessie hadn't checked out yet. As much as she hated to impose, her new friend was her only hope. If she could even still catch her.

After three rings, the hotel operator answered and Gina was promptly switched to someone who spoke English...impeccable English, in fact, and then, with a sinking heart, Gina replaced the receiver. There was no misunderstanding. No hope on which to cling. Jessie had checked out an hour ago.

Gina stared at the phone. She could call Nick. The thought made her prickle with a mixture of irritation and embarrassment. No way. That would be far too humiliating. She'd rather sleep on a park bench tonight, she thought, and made two more collect calls. After getting answering machines again, she gave up and trudged back around the corner to the main lobby.

Although it was probably near closing time, the lines were still long and the entire room sickeningly crowded. Seconds later, a guard locked the doors and she quickly got in line, hoping that she would at least be among the chosen few to get her business done today.

Taller than most of the people waiting in front of her, she idly glanced around the room while fanning herself, trying to find a distraction so that she didn't have to think about how stiflingly hot it was or how close everyone was pressed together.

In the right-hand corner, a mother was scolding her carrot-topped, red-faced young son. Beneath the large round wall clock, a pair of teenagers wearing backpacks held hands and made cow eyes at each other. Several yards away from them, a policeman was having words with someone.

Whatever the commotion was, it was attracting a number of onlookers. A minute later, another policeman joined the party, and then a third. The entire group started to get loud and there was a flash of handcuffs. A woman screamed, another angrily shouted something in Italian. A man started to break away from the group, and when one of the policemen tackled him, Gina was only mildly surprised to see it was the man who'd been annoying her earlier.

She craned her neck for a better look and watched him land with a thud across the floor, then slide to a stop not too far away from where she was standing. The startled people in front of her jumped apart, leaving a clear path between her and the spectacle on the floor.

The man tried to push himself up, but before he could make a getaway, the taller policeman slapped cuffs around the twerp's wrists. An eruption of angry Italian burst into the air.

Glancing at the wall clock, Gina frowned. Most people had scattered out of line and she thought about inching closer to the counter. Maybe the excitement had scared them off. Not her. She only hoped this little tussle didn't mean a delay.

With everyone else more interested in the goings-on and the orchestra of Italian reaching a loud crescendo, Gina cast a furtive look around and stepped closer to the counter. The paunchy middle-aged man on her left gave her a quizzical look. So did his reed-thin wife.

Gina sighed and stopped. It wasn't like she was cutting in line. It wasn't her fault everyone had chosen to rubberneck instead of keep their places.

It had gotten amazingly quiet all of a sudden, and when Gina glanced back at the couple they were still watching her. Someone briefly broke the silence by muttering something in Italian, which was most unnerving because she didn't understand a word of it. Nervous irritation made her shift from one foot to the other, and at the same time, she slid a look over her shoulder. Several more people were looking directly at her, condemnation tugging their faces into frowns.

With her luck, there was probably some strict law about line-cutting.

A sudden outburst of Italian once again disturbed the silence, making Gina jump and swivel toward the man being arrested.

His cuffed hands were in the air, pointing directly at her.

In the next instant, a pair of clunky silver bracelets complemented her startled indignation.

JACKSON SPRINTED UP the steps to police headquarters. As he pushed through the double doors, he ordered himself to calm down. He was angry, surprised, disappointed. He should have felt none of those things. Gina Hart was an American tourist, and therefore, strictly a business concern. At least he hoped she was simply an American tourist. The Italian police had a different story.

Irritated all over again, he stepped up to the reception desk and announced himself in Italian, explaining the reason for his presence.

The man behind the desk raised his bushy eyebrows in private amusement before calling for another officer from the back to escort Jackson.

When he started to question the older policeman as they walked down the narrow, dingy hall toward the back of the station, the gray-haired man grinned and said, "I understand English, *signore*. When I retire, we will go to America for a holiday. Please, we speak in English for my practice."

Reluctantly, Jackson nodded. However, he didn't want any misunderstandings. His Italian was perfect. If he received any indication that the man's English wasn't up to par, he would insist on reverting to Italian.

"You are, er, a friend of Signorina Hart?" the man asked, a sly grin tugging at his mouth, making his black mustache twitch. "Or here for embassy business?"

At the mention of Gina's name, two passing officers met his gaze and snickered.

He exhaled audibly. Well, so much for any misunderstanding. A part of him had hoped that charge against Gina had been a mistake. But the other man's meaning was clear, and so had been the lewd looks of the other two.

"She is in there." The officer motioned to another man to unlock the barred doors leading to a series of holding cells.

One short, swarthy man sat in the first cubicle. The second one was empty, but the third cell was crammed to capacity with an assortment of women, wearing anything from tight silver metallic pants to purple feather boas. In the middle, curled up on the floor, Gina sat braiding another woman's long blond hair.

Everyone was chattering or laughing or whining, mostly in Italian, with stray words of French and English thrown in, but as soon as the women saw him, all noise ceased. When Gina looked up, a dark flush spread across her cheeks.

She wove several more strands of hair, fastened them, then pushed to her feet. "I never thought I'd be glad to see you, Jack. I sure hope you speak Italian."

"Do you need me to interpret the charge against you?" he asked, but required no reply when her flush deepened.

"Oh-la-la." The redhead with the feather boa draped across her pale bare shoulders stepped up to the bars and beckoned him with one bright orange nail. "Is he yours, Gina?"

Jackson turned away, ignoring the chorus of giggles and suggestive smirks. His temper was already stretched to the limit, and disappointment pounded like a jackhammer in his head. "May I speak to her in private?" he asked the officer.

The man shrugged. "You can take her."

"Pardon me?"

"She is free to go with you."

"The charges have been dropped?" Jackson asked, hope renewing, and when the man frowned, he repeated his question in Italian.

Again, the officer shrugged. "The office of the police chief calls and tells me to do this. I do not ask questions."

Great. Jackson's secretary must have said something to the police chief's assistant when she rebooked their appointment. Now the police chief would figure Jackson owed him a favor. Just great. He turned toward Gina. "Are you ready?"

"You don't have to bite my head off. I didn't do anything." Her eyes holding his, she gave him a wounded look as the jailer unlocked the door.

Jackson said nothing. He stepped to the side to let her pass.

"Wait, Gina, don't forget this."

She turned to the blonde with the crisp British accent and smiled before accepting a piece of paper and stuffing it into her skirt pocket. "Thanks, Tracy. Hopefully I'll be on my way to Switzerland by tomorrow morning. But I'll still call the next time I'm in Rome."

God, but he hoped that wasn't soon. He put a hand at her elbow. She shifted away.

"I wouldn't count on going to Switzerland anytime soon," he said close to her ear. "This isn't over. Not by a long shot."

She lifted her chin and turned to glare at him. "Thanks, but I don't care to stick around for an apology."

Although her words were tart and edgy and filled with bravado, the hurt look still darkened her eyes, and Jackson suddenly wanted to kick himself for having already tried and convicted her. She didn't know the language. Maybe there *had* been a misunderstanding.

She needed the money, a small voice reminded him.

That didn't make her guilty.

Then he remembered the crack she'd made earlier about using her full name only when she got arrested. Sounded suspiciously like a common occurrence to him.

"We'll talk when we get back to the embassy," he said, and gripped her arm more firmly as he tried to usher her toward the hallway.

At the first cell where the man lay stretched out on a cot, Gina stopped and scowled at him. "You little worm. What the hell did you tell them?"

The man let his head fall to the side until he faced her, his expression unconcerned. Then he puckered his lips and tauntingly kissed the air in her direction.

"I'm gonna kill him," she said, lunging toward the bars.

Jackson grabbed her arm, swung her toward the hall and prodded her to move alongside him. "Good idea...threatening someone in a police station."

"Someone has to do something," she said, straining against his hold.

He held firm and kept pulling her along toward the front of the station, hoping they could reach his car without further incident.

Several passing policemen grinned at Gina and bid her farewell by name. She smiled back and returned their goodbyes, using each of their first names, as well. Obviously, she'd made quite an impression, which did nothing to lighten his mood.

As soon as they were alone, her smile disappeared. "For your information, Jack, I did not want you to be

called. Because I'm American they insisted you be no-
tified.''

"And how were you planning to get released?"

"I'm innocent. I shouldn't have been arrested in the
first place. That guy lied about me."

"What did he say?"

"How should I know? I don't speak Italian well
enough."

He slowed once they left the station and stared down
at her. "You do know what the charges were."

"Yeah." She rolled her eyes and jerked away from
him. "Solicitation." She dusted off her sleeve as though
his hold had somehow soiled her. "Well, thanks for
getting me out."

"You weren't, were you?"

He regretted the words as soon as they left his mouth.
When he met her startled gaze and saw pain replace her
shock, his regret turned to grief. She was never going
to forgive him for asking her that question.

She folded her arms across her chest. "Selling myself?"

Damn. "Get in the car." He motioned toward his
low-slung red sports car parked at the curb five feet
away.

"Thanks, but I can find my own way back."

"Get in, Gina." His voice was tight and low, and
when she didn't so much as blink, he wondered if she'd
heard him above the blaring horns and the chattering
pedestrians passing them in hordes.

"So it's Gina now, huh?" She shrugged, her arms
still folded. "Yeah, I guess bailing me out puts us on
familiar ground."

"Could we please continue this discussion in the
car?" He opened the door for her.

"No, thanks, Jack. I'll see you in the morning."

When she started to turn away, he caught her arm. "This isn't multiple choice. You're in my custody."

Twilight had settled in, casting gray shadows down the sidewalk and across her face. But he didn't need to see her expression to know that she was hurt and angry. Too bad. He wasn't happy about having his evening ruined, either.

"I didn't hear them say any such thing," she said, shaking free but staying put. "You didn't even have to fill out any paperwork."

"Look, the police chief is a friend of mine. He's obviously released you as a personal favor, and he expects that I'll account for you. That's what I'm doing." He was stretching the truth. They weren't personal friends, and he had no idea what Gianni Martinelli expected of him. But he had no intention of letting Gina roam around with no place to go. No matter how irritated she was with him, or he with her.

"I just don't want to be any trouble," she said, but the stubborn angle of her chin was already starting to soften.

"Right."

Her chin went back up, and she let out an exasperated snort.

"I'm sorry. That was uncalled for." He stopped and sniffed the air. The aroma of roasted garlic chicken drifted through the air from the bistro across the street. "Did they feed you in there?"

"No. You sprung me before dinner. Damn it."

He hid a smile. "Then the least I can do is feed you myself."

She blinked, her defensive posture relaxing slightly.

"I'll pay you back every cent as soon as I get my money."

"Don't worry about it." He gestured toward the open car door. "I have a place in mind."

She wouldn't budge except to hold out her hand. "I'd like a piece of paper, please."

He frowned. "Can we do this later?"

"No."

Shaking his head, he reached into his inside breast pocket and withdrew a small leather-bound notebook. After tearing out a sheet, he handed it to her.

"Pen?"

His patience on the wane, he passed her that, too, then motioned toward the passenger seat. "Now, will you get in?"

She briefly eyed the black Mont Blanc pen with mocking interest, then sat at the edge of the tan leather car seat and swung her long legs inside. From behind him, a man whistled.

The attention did not make Gina happy. She glared past Jackson toward the source of the sound before facing straight ahead with an oddly prim expression on her face. Once he joined her inside the car, he saw that she'd torn the paper in half and was scribbling something under the dim overhead light.

She folded one piece and scrawled something more on the other. "Here," she said, holding out the first half.

He took it. In bold letters, she'd written an IOU.

"You can fill in the amount later," she said, and settled back against the leather seats. "I trust you."

He smiled and started the engine. "Okay." He wasn't going to argue with her, even though he had no intention of collecting. "Let's stop at the embassy and pick up your clothes."

Her interest was obviously peaked. She straightened. "Actually, I would like to take a shower before eating. Is that possible?"

"Absolutely."

She relaxed again. "Are there facilities at the embassy?"

At a break in traffic, he pulled the sports car into the street. "You can take a shower at my apartment," he said, glancing at her and pausing to meet her narrowed gaze. "You'll be staying with me tonight."

Chapter Five

Gina had already pretty much figured out Jack was rich just by the way he spoke and carried himself. His brand of confidence wasn't bought or learned, it was bred. She just hadn't understood how rich he was, she realized as she eyed the recently set dining room table.

The petite, ebony-haired maid flicked her gaze curiously at Gina as she set down brandy snifters near the wineglasses, all Waterford crystal, unless Gina missed her guess. Beneath royal blue plates trimmed and monogrammed in gold was a tablecloth made of Belgian linen finer than Gina had ever seen.

And she'd seen plenty. That's what she liked about her courier job. It took her places and exposed her to things she'd never thought possible while growing up in her Brooklyn neighborhood.

The dining room table was antique oak, massive, and had probably been passed down from one generation to the next. She'd half expected to find the two settings placed formally at opposite ends, but instead, the maid had set the head of the table and the spot to the right, and she'd purposely moved a Limoges vase of fresh flowers into a more intimate position closer to the settings.

The entire scene looked cozy. Too cozy.

"I hope you found everything you needed," Jack said from behind her.

Gina turned toward his voice and watched him enter the dining room. He'd changed into a pair of gray slacks and a white polo shirt. Somehow, on him, the clothes still didn't look very casual. "Are you kidding? You have more stuff in that bathroom than most five-star hotels."

He looked bewildered for a moment. "Good. I leave that up to Isabella." He smiled at the maid and said something in Italian.

Gina didn't know a lot of the language, only what she'd picked up as a kid from her grandmother and from her past courier trips, but she knew enough to tell that he not only thanked the woman but suggested she sleep late tomorrow. There was a little more, enough to make the woman blush as she headed out, but Gina didn't understand it.

She glared suspiciously at him.

He frowned back. "You don't mind that we serve ourselves, do you? Isabella has stayed past her appointed time and she has her two grandchildren waiting at home."

Gina laughed. "Yeah, Jack, I think we could probably manage to serve ourselves."

He gave her an odd look. She sighed. Obviously he didn't see the humor in his remark.

"I'll be right back," he said. "I'm going to bring the serving dishes in from the kitchen."

"That's ridiculous." She followed him as he headed toward the door to the kitchen. When he stopped, she pushed him from behind to keep going, and was surprised to find how solid he felt. This was a man who worked out. The idea startled her.

"What are you doing?" he asked over his shoulder. His face was close, his warm breath caressing her cheek like a sultry summer breeze.

She dropped her hands and immediately put some distance between them. "We're going to save some dishes and fill our plates up from the stove."

"Why?"

"Because." For an instant, she couldn't think. Flickering candlelight coming from the oak buffet did tricky things to his blue eyes. Below all that thick dark hair, they looked entirely too seductive and were trained intensely on her. "Don't you believe in saving water?" she asked. "Besides, I'm too hungry to wait." She flapped her hands at him to get him moving again.

"If that's what you want."

He preceded her into the kitchen, where, the air absorbed the mouth-watering aroma of tomatoes and roasted meat like a sponge sucked up water. Her stomach growled with unabashed hunger.

She saw one side of Jack's mouth lift, but he said nothing as he started uncovering the pots. Gina started to help him but was surprised to see that he wasn't having any trouble finding his way around the kitchen.

He went unerringly into a drawer and withdrew a quilted yellow mitt, then pulled a tray of rolls from the oven. After setting them aside, he got out individual salads, butter and wine from the refrigerator.

Glancing over at her, he nudged his head in the direction of the stove. "Go ahead and start." Then, misreading her hesitation, he added, "If you don't want to use those wooden cooking spoons, there are some silver serving ones in the drawer on your left."

"No, these are fine." *Well, well.* She smiled to herself. She would have bet her return plane ticket home that old Jackson Maxwell Covington III wouldn't have known squat about where to find anything.

He further amazed her by starting to whistle while he carried their salads into the dining room and continuing while he returned with their plates. "Guess we need these," he said, something close to a grin tugging at his mouth...his attractive mouth. His way too attractive mouth.

"Yeah." She took the plate, feeling slightly dazed. Was she nuts? It was impossible for her to be the least bit attracted to this man. Not one ounce. Nada. Zip. Hadn't she just learned her lesson with Nick?

"Are you okay?"

"No, I'm not okay. I'm hungry. All I've had since last night is half a pound of chocolate." She vented her sudden frustration by digging wholeheartedly into the first pot, and the assortment of heavenly smells instantly conspired to distract her.

"A half a pound of chocolate?" He stopped uncorking the wine and stared at her in disbelief. "No wonder you felt sick."

She sighed. She hadn't meant to reveal that tidbit. "I had no money, only a leftover bribe. Did you want me to starve?"

His gaze narrowed. "What kind of bribe? For whom?"

She was really putting her foot in it tonight. No way was she going to tell him about Nick and what a fool she'd been. She'd go back to jail first. "It was a joke. I brought chocolates for a friend. But the joke ended up being on me, okay? Are you going to eat before this gets cold?"

"I thought you didn't have any friends here with you."

"Turns out I didn't." She looked him straight in the eye, daring him to question her further.

"We're having veal. Is red wine all right with you?"

Her stomach rolled at the thought of any more wine. The revulsion must have shown in her face because he quickly said, "Maybe your stomach isn't up to anything alcoholic. I'll set out some bottled water."

"I'd appreciate it," she said, and finished dishing herself up. "Do you want me to fix your plate?"

"No, thanks. Go sit down. I'll be right behind you."

He was good to his word. Before she'd opened her eyes from reciting the little chant she'd made up to help her remember which utensil to use when, he was setting down his plate.

She looked at it and laughed. "No wonder you didn't want me to get that for you."

He glanced down at his plate, then gazed at hers and frowned. "I don't like my food mushed together."

She continued to stare at his dinner, mesmerized by the fastidious arrangement of food, organized almost to the point of being color coordinated. "Did you go to art class to learn how to do that?"

He lifted his linen napkin off the table and opened it with an annoyed snap before laying it across his lap, then eyed her food again. The fragrant tomato sauce spilled from the fettucine onto the meat, and the grilled baby vegetables were barely discernible under a mound of grated cheese. The entire meal looked like it had been slapped on the plate by a passing hurricane.

"And you being the gourmand that you are should criticize me?" he asked, and picked up his fork with attitude.

"Chill out, Jack, I'm only teasing you." She grinned. "But I believe you picked up the salad fork."

He stared at the utensil, his jaw slackening as if he couldn't believe he'd made such a faux pas. Or maybe he didn't think she knew the difference.

The notion tweaked her pride. Annoyed, she stabbed a piece of veal, put it in her mouth and chewed.

He put the fork down and sipped his wine. After he returned the goblet to the table, he said, "Don't call me Jack."

"What should I call you?"

"Jackson is fine."

"It sounds too formal."

"It's my name."

She forked up some pasta and twirled it around a baby carrot before she put the combination in her mouth. His gaze flicked distastefully her way before he started on his salad.

"Okay," she said, suddenly losing pleasure in her meal. That one small glance had set her off, and now she battled her dread of feeling "less than." "You have a right to be called what you want."

He nodded. "How's your dinner?"

"Great," she said, despite her dented enthusiasm. "Did you cook it?"

He shook his head, clearly oblivious to her teasing. "I only cook on Saturdays and Sundays when Isabella is off."

"You *do* cook?" She leaned back to stare at him. "Well, color me surprised."

"Why should you be? I eat. I'd better know how to cook."

"Somehow, I can't see you in an apron."

"And you won't." A slow curve of his mouth lifted

his lips in an attractive smile. It reached his eyes, and played havoc with her nervous system.

"Maybe I will have a touch of that wine," she said, picking up her glass and presenting it to him.

His fingers brushed hers as he took it, and Gina bit her lip to keep from snatching back her hand and making a complete fool of herself. He might as well have thrown her backward over his arm and kissed her silly for all the tingling that one little innocent touch caused.

"Go easy on this," he said, handing the goblet back to her. "Make sure it won't make you sick before you drink too much."

"I don't think I should stay here tonight," she blurted.

Bewildered, questioning, his eyes met hers. "Did I miss something here?"

"No." *Apparently.* "I just think we should get that straight right away so I can make other arrangements."

He laid down his fork and leaned back in his chair. "Such as?"

"You let me worry about that."

He studied her for a long moment, until the silence verged on uncomfortable. Then he said, "You're still upset because I thought you were a hooker."

"Nope. You don't know me. I can understand how the arrest looked." The lie was a small one. On the one hand she truly did understand, but on the other she was ticked that he could think such a thing. She was disappointed, too, although there was no logic to her feeling.

"I'm glad you can appreciate my position. You're right, of course, I don't know you. I only knew you needed money, and—" He cut himself short, his expression turning wary, and he shook his head, causing her to tingle with unease.

"What were you going to say?"

"It's not important."

"Then tell me."

His sigh was loud and filled with frustration. "That I'm sorry I jumped to a wrong conclusion."

"Bull." She held his gaze, knowing without a doubt that he wanted to look away. "You didn't jump to any conclusions. You simply reacted to the facts presented to you. What were you really going to say?"

"Can't we drop this and have a nice dinner?"

"No, *Jackson*, we can't. I want to know what you were going to say." She laid down her fork so that she could clasp her shaky hands together in her lap.

The trembling meant her temper was rising, which made her angrier. And although she could well end up being the poster child for jumping to conclusions, she had a deep and disturbing feeling that she wasn't going to like whatever he was going to say.

"I'm not sure how I can explain without making you mad." His expression was blank, maybe even dispassionate, and she promised herself she could be an adult about this because he was right—they didn't know each other. And no way would she give him the power to upset her.

"Try me," she said. "I'm a reasonable person."

"Okay." He looked her straight in the eyes. "Your clothes."

"My clothes?" She lifted her brows, uncomprehending. "What about my clothes?"

He didn't want to explain further. That was clear in every tensed muscle in his face. But she gave him credit for still not looking away.

He cleared his throat. "The way you dress...well, it's not exactly considered office attire."

"I don't work in an office."

"Touché." One side of his mouth lifted in a wry half smile.

She let a moment of silence stretch, pondering how deep the arrow he'd just slung went. But all she felt was slightly numb. Disappointment affected her like that sometimes.

"So, you think I look sleazy?" she asked finally, proud of how calm and composed she sounded.

"No. I didn't say that." Anger tinged his voice.

"You implied it."

"Then I apologize."

"Okay, Mr. Covington, I'll give you the benefit of the doubt. Tell me exactly what you meant."

He briefly closed his eyes and sighed with loud frustration. "Come on, Gina."

She had no reason to let him off the hook. Except if she pushed any harder, he'd know that he'd hurt her feelings. "Okay, forget it. No problem."

"I've hurt your feelings. I'm sorry."

She sniffed. "You think way too highly of yourself," she said, picking up her fork and taking a small bite, not because she had any appetite left, but because she needed something to do. "I'd have to care about your opinion in the first place in order for you to be able to do that."

He half smiled, and she thought she saw a trace of pity in his eyes. "Look, you're an attractive woman—"

"Don't." She dropped her fork and held up a hand. "You do a very bad tap dance, Jackson. You were right. Let's drop it." Then she pushed back from the table, prepared to return her half-filled plate to the kitchen.

He put out a hand. "You haven't finished your dinner."

"I took too much. I'm sorry for wasting it."

"I don't care about that. I just don't want—"

"Of course you don't care about that." She barked a short, humorless laugh, while sweeping a gaze around the opulent room. "Why should you?" Her eyes came back to meet his. "It's clear you've never been without anything. I bet you have a spare toothbrush ready before the old one wears out."

His brows drew together over narrowed eyes, darkening with bewilderment. "I'm not sure what's going on here. I know you think I've insulted you, and if I have, that's unforgivable, but I'd appreciate a chance to explain."

"No need," she said with a cheery wave of her hand. She even managed a brief smile before picking up her plate and turning toward the kitchen.

"You're right," he said after a moment of silence.

She'd already made it to the kitchen door, but she paused, damn her inquisitive nature. Angling around, she asked, "Right about what?"

He shrugged. "I've had everything I've ever wanted."

A smug smile threatened the corners of her mouth, although she would have preferred if he'd at least look apologetic. "That's pretty obvious, Jackson."

"I don't know how. I've worked hard for everything I've ever received."

"Yeah, right," she said with a dismissive roll of her eyes.

"Oh, I see." He stood and started gathering up the rest of the plates, his posture one of extreme nonchalance. "You aren't tolerant of someone else jumping to conclusions, but you don't mind taking the leap."

She blinked. "Leave my wine on the table. I'll be back for it," she said, and disappeared behind the gleaming white door.

As soon as she disposed of the remains of her food and set her plate in the huge, spotless sink, she slumped against the marble counter. She was right about him. She knew she was. The real question was, what did it matter? Why were her emotions doing this zigzag routine? She was overtired, and after starving all afternoon, she really should have forced herself to eat more, but something else was interfering with her good sense.

Maybe it was because watching him in the kitchen earlier had disarmed her. She hadn't expected to see that side of him. And just maybe she'd hoped...

It doesn't matter, you idiot, she scolded herself. *You live in different poles.* Besides, hadn't she only yesterday sworn off men? Jessie and Libby would throttle her if they knew she had the slightest tinge of longing....

The door swung open, and she immediately straightened before he appeared. His hands were full, one salad plate actually balanced on the spot above his wrist, and in spite of herself, she chuckled.

His solemn gaze flicked to hers.

Trying to lose the smile, she said, "You look like a professional waiter."

Without spilling a single morsel, he slid the plates onto the counter, then turned one lifted brow in her direction. He said nothing, but his expression plainly said, "Not bad for someone who's never lifted a finger in his life, huh?"

She pursed her mouth, refusing to sulk. It wasn't in her nature, but she wasn't going to apologize, either.

After all, she hadn't insulted *him*. It wasn't his fault he'd had a silver spoon waiting for him.

After a brief silence, he turned away to scrape the food off the plates, and she stared down at her pink-tipped toes. This particular polish was a little too bright, even for her, but when she'd gotten the pedicure two days ago, she'd been running late all day, trying to get ready for her big trip to Rome, and she'd opted not to change the color.

It had been her fault for not paying attention to what the manicurist was doing. Gina had been too busy day-dreaming about what a great time she and Nick were going to have.

She snorted softly, sliding Jack a covert sidelong look when the sound came out too loud. Man, between anticipation of the trip and the lousy reunion she'd had with Nick, she'd been in left field for nearly a week now. No wonder her nerves were as jittery as a bridegroom's at the twelfth hour.

She curled her toes over the edge of her sandals until the polished tips were nearly out of sight, then stared at her knees. Jack had been good enough to stop by the embassy to pick up her suitcases on the way to his place, and although she'd changed after her shower, she'd replaced her previous short skirt with yet another.

Her legs weren't bad, and the hem wasn't indecently short. Her ribbed, scoop-neck T-shirt was in fashion. Lots of women wore them. And although her grandmother might tend to agree with Jackson, no way did Gina look like a hooker. Just because she couldn't afford Armani suits...

"Isabella made dessert, and I'm going to make some coffee. Are you interested?" Jack asked, without looking at her. He opened the dishwasher door and started loading it.

"Hey, I can do that." Gina pushed away from the counter. No matter how irritated she was with him, he was being gracious about housing and feeding her. The least she could do was her share.

"I can manage."

He spoke the three simple words evenly and without any expression on his face, but in that instant, Gina knew she'd hurt his feelings, too. The idea was preposterous. But way down deep in her gut, she knew it was true. Her instinct was rarely wrong.

"I don't doubt that," she said. "I just want to help."

"Then you can make the coffee. I believe Isabella ground some before she left. You'll find it in the container near the espresso machine."

Her gaze followed the nudge of his chin to the corner of the long black-and-white-marble countertop. The series of spotless stainless-steel appliances lined up against the white-tiled backsplash gleamed so brightly from Isabella's elbow grease that it gave Gina a headache.

Woodenly, she moved to the espresso machine and measured some grounds. "I spoke hastily before," she said, keeping her eyes on what she was doing and away from his. "I appreciate you putting me up tonight. In fact, if you don't mind, I think I'll skip joining you for coffee and dessert. I'm really tired."

"I understand." He closed the dishwasher door with a thud. "Of course, Isabella showed you your room."

Gina exhaled slowly. That was easy. "She did."

"Good." He moved beside her. Close. She could smell his mysterious musky scent. One large hand covered hers.

She stilled, and he took the silver scoop from her fingers.

"Go on," he said. "Get some rest."

"Thanks." She slipped away but couldn't shake the warmth of his touch.

"Gina?" he called, and she paused by the door and looked into eyes that were suddenly cold and dark. "I'll do everything I can to get you on that plane to Switzerland tomorrow."

Chapter Six

"I don't understand what the holdup is, Greta." Jackson twirled his Mont Blanc pen from one finger to the next, then back again while he balanced the phone receiver against his shoulder and leaned way back in his chair, away from his desk. "I'll pay for Ms. Hart's passport."

He frowned at the phone. "Hello? Greta? Hello? Hello?"

He slammed the receiver down with a vicious curse. That was the second time today he'd been cut off from her.

His secretary chose that very moment to walk into his office, and judging by the shocked look on her face, she'd obviously heard the uncharacteristic word he'd used. He exhaled loudly. "Are we having trouble with the phone lines today?"

Marcy wrinkled her freckled nose. "Not that I'm aware of. I'll call the operator and check."

"Never mind." His restless gaze wandered to the folder in her hand. "You have something for me?"

"I have some RSVPs to answer once you tell me whether you'll be attending any of these functions." She passed the folder to him. "Couldn't you sleep last night?"

A pain was settling right between his brows, and he squinted up at her. "Why?"

"I don't know. You seem edgy." Her gaze settled on the pen he continued to twirl between his fingers.

He tried to stop the motion, but the pen ended up flipping into the air. He caught it before it hit the floor, but the cap flew off and black ink from the cartridge sprayed the air, splattering his crisp white shirt.

He stared down at his chest, appalled at the mess such a small amount of ink could make. "I don't believe this."

Marcy's wide-eyed gaze switched from his shirt to his face. "The cartridge must have gotten loose."

No kidding. He kept the sarcastic remark to himself. "Do me a favor and check my coat closet. There may be some shirts from the cleaners in there I haven't taken home yet."

Mutely, she did as he asked, then turned and shook her head. "You want me to run over to your place? Isabella can give me a fresh shirt."

He passed a hand over his face and blew a frustrated breath into his palm. Moving his hand away, he gave Marcy a weary smile. "Thanks, anyway, but I'll take care of it. You figure out which of those functions I need to attend, then RSVP. Half the time you know more about these things than I do."

Marcy flushed. "Don't exaggerate, although I'll be sure to remind you of that when it's time for my raise."

Glancing at his calendar, he chuckled. "I won't be long. My next appointment isn't until eleven. I'll return before then."

She handed him his suit coat off the valet near the closet. "Do you want me to order in lunch? Or do you have other plans?"

He instantly thought of Gina and wondered if she was awake yet. "Hold off for now." He had trouble meeting Marcy's eyes. Which was totally absurd. So what if he wanted to keep his schedule open? He was trying to get Gina on that plane to Switzerland, wasn't he? He leveled his gaze with Marcy's. "I'll let you know before noon."

"Okay. Anything else you want me to do while you're gone?"

He strode to the door while shrugging into his jacket. "Yeah. Find out flight times to Zurich. Say, anything after three-thirty." Surely Greta would have gotten Gina's paperwork ironed out by then.

"For one or two people?"

He gave her an odd look. She stared back, unblinking. It was a logical question. She didn't even know who the ticket was for. Why the hell was he being so touchy this morning?

He knew why. He'd hated the way he and Gina had left things last night. And it was his fault for bringing up the way she dressed. There had been no reason for it. But if her being arrested wasn't enough, what was he supposed to think when he arrived at the police station and along with her short skirt, her blouse had been tied up to expose her bare midriff? Still, that was no excuse for insulting her. But she had a knack for setting him off balance.

Marcy tilted her head expectantly, and he realized she was awaiting an answer from him about the number of tickets required.

He took a second to gather his thoughts. "Only one."

"Consider it done," she said as she preceded him out of the office. "I'll check on the phone problem, too."

"Thanks. And tell Greta I'd appreciate her making Ms. Hart's paperwork a priority."

Traffic was relatively light this time of the morning, and he made it to his apartment in good time. It probably hadn't hurt that he'd run two red lights along the way. He shook his head as he unfolded himself from his car, wondering what had him so distracted.

As soon as he let himself into the apartment, Isabella took one look at his ink-splattered shirt and went scurrying to his bedroom suite before he could ask her about Gina.

He slipped out of his jacket and strolled toward the kitchen while tugging off his tie. Except for half a pot of coffee being kept warm, everything was in place, the room spotless, offering no clue as to whether Gina had recently eaten. He went on to the dining room and found everything in order there, as well.

He stopped in the living room. Nothing amiss, except he noticed that Isabella had started rearranging the furniture in anticipation of the Victorian walnut side chair they were expecting. But still no sign of Gina.

He frowned. The apartment was quiet, too quiet, and he got a sudden uneasy feeling that maybe she'd slipped away to go do God knows what.

"Isabella," he called out, while unbuttoning his shirt and heading for his room.

Just as he passed the guest room, the door opened. He stopped and turned in time to see Gina stifle a yawn. Her hair was sleep-tousled, several long strands clinging to her cheeks, her bangs sticking out in two comical directions. She reared back, startled, then quickly patted down her bangs, blinking at him as though she were trying to focus.

"Mornin'," she mumbled, then put a hand to her mouth to cover another yawn.

Try as he might to stop it, his gaze slipped to her bare shoulders, her scantily covered chest. A piece of very sheer pink dipped low into her cleavage and scarcely sheathed two very pert nipples.

He hardened immediately. Cursing himself, he forced his attention to her face. He was a normal, red-blooded thirty-seven-year-old man. There was absolutely no reason for him not to react. Now, he had to get the hell out of here.

"Isabella has some coffee made. She'll fix you breakfast when you're ready," he said, but Gina, suddenly wide-eyed, stepped back and slammed the door before he got the last word out.

Gina took extra care in getting ready, making sure she put on the only pair of slacks she'd brought with her, and despising herself every minute for caving in even the slightest bit. There was nothing wrong with the way she dressed. If Jack didn't like the way she looked, tough cookies.

Taking a final glance at herself in the mirror before leaving the room, she sighed. Maybe she was taking so much care in order to prolong the inevitable.

She wasn't looking forward to facing him again.

She'd been disoriented earlier, still groggy from sleep, when she'd opened her door to find herself, quite literally, face-to-face with him. Heck, chest-to-chest with him was more like it. And what a nice chest he had, too. His unbuttoned shirt had given her a pulse-racing gander of firm muscle, dark, silky hair and enough temptation to humble a saint.

Not that Gina could claim such a title. Although she

wasn't quite as racy as many people gave her credit for, she definitely was experienced enough to understand the look he gave her. Her only consolation was that it had seemed to have scared the hell out of him as much as it had her.

It didn't matter, she further consoled herself. Within a few hours, she'd be making tracks out of Rome. Out of Italy. Away from Jackson Maxwell Covington III.

The hall was clear and she hesitated, trying to figure out if she was supposed to turn right or left to get to the kitchen. Given a map she was fine, but she had the most miserable sense of direction without one.

She heard a noise that sounded like pots clanging, so she headed in that direction. An unidentifiable but delicious smell lured her farther but reminded her of the half-eaten dinner she'd abandoned and what had caused her to lose her appetite.

Nice chest or not, she sincerely hoped she'd taken long enough to get ready that Jackson had already left for the embassy. Her watch had stopped some time early last evening, but she could tell by the amount of bright sunlight glutting her room and the hall that it was on the late side.

She frowned. She hoped not too late. Time wasn't something she could afford to waste.

The aroma of ham and eggs intensified right before Gina rounded the corner into the kitchen. She was going to kiss Isabella, then buy her a big bouquet of flowers as soon as she got some money.

Jack stood at the stove with a spatula in his hand. He flipped over a golden brown omelet before glancing at her. "Your timing couldn't be better," he said.

He looked unperturbed, as though they hadn't faced each other seminaked only forty-five minutes ago, but he switched his gaze back to the stove too quickly, letting her know he wasn't quite as unaffected as he pretended.

"Where's Isabella?" she asked, her tone edgy.

Judging by the wary look on his face, he'd noticed. "She had to step away for a minute," he said, then inclined his head toward the refrigerator. "Help yourself to some fruit."

She poured herself a cup of coffee instead. "What time do you leave for work?"

He turned off the stove and gave her a puzzled look. "I've already been to the embassy. I came back to change my shirt."

Her gaze flew to the wall clock and she let out a shriek. "It's ten-thirty?" Angry, she turned back to him and repeated, "Ten-thirty! How could you let me sleep so late?"

"You obviously needed the rest. Besides, Greta is still working on getting you a new passport."

"You lose a passport, you get a replacement the same day. Read any travel book." She slid her coffee cup onto the counter. In her excitement, she'd taken a sip too fast and burned her tongue. Now, with her hands free, she waved them in the air. "What is the problem?"

His dark brows dipped in a frown as if he didn't know the answer. "Well, first you got sick, then you got arrested."

"Don't start," she warned. "Those things should have nothing to do with handling my paperwork."

She was right. She could tell by his reticent expression, although he didn't say so. Instead he replied, "Eat before your omelet gets cold." Using the spatula, he scooped up the folded eggs and slid them onto a plate, then handed it to her. "I have to get back to the office. I'll send someone by for you later."

Tearing her longing gaze away from the plate, she said, "Don't you dare leave without me."

"I can't wait. I have a meeting at eleven."

"I'll come with you now."

"Isabella made you that omelet." He handed her a fork. "She just ran to the corner to get you fresh warm bread."

Gina gritted her teeth. He wasn't playing fair. She didn't want to have put the maid out for nothing.

The distant sound of the entry door opening made her glance over her shoulder before she leaned against the counter and sighed, suddenly feeling every bit as tired as when she'd crawled into bed last night. The woman had actually gone out of her way to get fresh bread. How could Gina thumb her nose at the offering? Especially since, according to Jack, she had no good reason to do so. Her paperwork was still being handled. But of course…she could try to hurry them….

Isabella appeared at the door, slightly out of breath, a loaf of fragrant bread in her hands, and Gina returned her earnest smile, knowing she didn't have the heart to disappoint the woman.

"She really went all the way to the corner, huh" she whispered to Jack.

He nodded.

"What time will you send someone?" she asked Jack, trying not to sound peevish.

A slow smile curved his lips, and something she could foolishly mistake for admiration glinted in his eyes.

HE SHOULD HAVE LET Marcy order him lunch. Gina was going to arrive at any minute, and Jackson knew she'd recently eaten. It had been easy getting her to stay behind and eat the breakfast Isabella had prepared. So easy that it had amazed him.

Sitting here at his desk an hour and a half later, he still felt a little surprised. Miranda wouldn't have thought twice about going on with her business no matter who she inconvenienced. In her mind, fixing breakfast was Isabella's job; whether Miranda ate it or not didn't matter. Of course, Miranda had grown up being waited on. It probably never occurred to her that sometimes her behavior appeared selfish.

Jackson shifted uncomfortably. Was he that bad, too? He thanked Isabella for nearly every meal she cooked him. And he was generous with her grandchildren at birthdays and Christmas. The same with Marcy's kids. Plus, he paid Isabella a salary far above scale, and gave Marcy a bonus at Christmas out of his own pocket. Still, he often took them both for granted. He knew that now. He just hadn't thought about it before.

When the limo driver had called a half hour ago to tell Jackson that he'd be late bringing Gina to the embassy because she'd insisted on washing the linen she'd used last night, Jackson's initial reaction had been one of irritation. But the annoyance had soon petered into self-examination and finally, respect. Now he was back to self-recrimination.

He stood abruptly, a decision made, and walked out of his office. Marcy was on the phone, so he scribbled her a brief note and continued downstairs. A relief person was sitting at Greta's desk, so he kept walking down the hall. He'd already left two messages for her, and he was starting to think she was avoiding him.

Which made no sense, so he chalked up his paranoia to a sleepless night.

He had scarcely stepped foot into the embassy cafeteria when several pairs of startled eyes turned his way. The room was large, hosting several rows of tables covered with cream-colored tablecloths, although only half of them were occupied. When the whispering started, he turned his head and continued on to the service line. At least he hoped that's where he was going. He'd never eaten here before. When he didn't have a lunch appointment somewhere in town, Marcy usually ordered his lunch and it was served in his office.

He smiled at the short, plump woman behind the counter and she blushed clear to the roots of her sandy-blond hair, tucked tightly into a black hairnet. "Do I order here?" he asked.

She nodded, tilted slightly to the side and let her gaze drift past him, her wide eyes sending a secret signal to someone.

He knew better than to turn around. The place had already quieted considerably. Which was totally absurd. Surely his presence in the cafeteria wasn't that big a deal.

"How about a turkey sandwich?" he asked, anxious suddenly to get back to his office. "To go."

She swung around, and he watched her make the sloppy french bread sandwich. He would have preferred a croissant, and he wasn't crazy about the alfalfa sprouts she added, but he was more interested in her efficiency and his departure.

After he'd paid the woman and made his way to the door, he caught sight of Greta sitting in the corner, sipping a cup of coffee, her thoughtful gaze fastened on him. As much as he wanted to get out of here, he needed to corner Greta more. But as soon as he approached her, she stood. He frowned, wondering if the reason she hadn't flagged him down was because she was in a hurry.

"Have you got a minute?" he asked.

"Just one."

"I'll walk you out."

She looked as though she wanted to refuse, then gave him a tight smile and preceded him out the door.

Greta wasn't acting at all like herself, and it was starting to grate on him. Of course, he wasn't acting normal, either.

He waited until the door was closed behind him and they were alone in the hall. "Why didn't you motion to me when I came in?"

She glanced at him with a look of amusement on her face. "I was shocked speechless to see you down here."

He gave her a wry smile. "All right. Point taken. Now, what's the status of Ms. Hart's passport?"

"I was going to come up and see you about that after lunch."

"Gee, it's my turn to be shocked."

"What's that supposed to mean?" she asked, slanting him an unconcerned look.

Two secretaries from upstairs were coming head-on, and since the hall was too narrow to accommodate all four of them, Jackson hung back for a moment. He nodded as they passed, then had to hurry to catch up with Greta, who obviously had no intention of waiting for him.

"What's going on that you're so busy?" he asked once he'd positioned himself abreast from her.

"I'm always busy, Mr. Covington."

That did it. She never called him Mr. Covington in

private. "Is there something you want to discuss, *Ms. Morgan?* Is there a problem here?"

She chuckled. "Look, there's Gina at the top of the stairs. Go make sure she doesn't get arrested or something, and I'll be up as soon as I ask my relief to continue to cover for me." Ever efficient, Greta turned away and started picking up the accumulated pink message slips off her desk.

That was the thing. She was one of the most efficient people he knew. He didn't understand what was holding up Gina's new passport.

The relief receptionist sitting at Greta's desk said something to make Greta laugh again, and Jackson stared for another moment, considering how pretty Greta was when she either laughed or smiled. She did neither often enough, yet she looked much younger when she did. She was only two years older than he, and they'd been fairly good friends for a long time. What he appreciated most about her was that she was a good sport about attending embassy dinners with him when Miranda was out of town, which was a more frequent occurrence these days. But even before he'd met Miranda, he and Greta had never shared a romantic interest. He wondered why.

Her phone rang, the noise breaking into his reverie and reminding him that Gina was on the loose somewhere upstairs. He motioned a reminder for Greta to come up to his office, not sure she even saw him, then ascended the stairs at a brisk pace.

Gina was on his couch sipping a cup of tea and chatting with Marcy when he arrived. His secretary didn't usually socialize much with her co-workers, and she straightened as soon as she saw him.

"Can I get you anything?" she asked him, and when he shook his head, she promptly let herself out.

He turned to Gina. "I'm glad to see you making yourself at home."

A dull rose color seeped into her complexion and she lifted her chin. "Ms. Morgan wasn't at her desk, and Marcy invited me into your office."

He immediately regretted the defensiveness he'd caused. She'd be gone in a couple of hours. He wanted them to part on good terms. "No, I'm glad you're here. You can keep me company while I eat my lunch."

"I'd rather be boarding a plane." She set the delicate china cup and saucer on the coffee table, then looked up at him. "I'm afraid I owe you for a phone call to New York. I had to call my brother again. Isabella assured me it was all right."

"No problem. I'll charge you interest," he said, and chuckled when she gave him a double-take.

A grin tugged at the corners of her mouth. "My brother was a little short on cash, and he didn't have much to send me. Will you trust me to send you a check?"

"Depends. What kind of collateral are we talking about?" He sat behind his desk and unwrapped his sandwich. He didn't want it anymore, but he needed the distraction.

She looked especially appealing this morning, with her hair freshly washed and gleaming. Her makeup was sparse, just enough to accent her almond-shaped eyes and high cheekbones.

Today her clothes were much more conservative. This morning he'd barely noticed how tailored her navy blue slacks were, or how her white cotton blouse revealed few of her generous curves. She looked nice, well groomed, but damn it, he missed her legs. Incredibly, he missed her ridiculous short skirt.

She leaned back, confident, maybe even a little smug, her brown eyes beginning to sparkle with mischief. "What sort of collateral did you want?"

Jackson recognized a no-win situation when he saw one. No matter what he said, she'd tried to best him, or worse yet, twist his words around. "I was only teasing. Of course you were free to use my phone."

Something looking suspiciously like disappointment chased the twinkle from her eyes. Shaking her head, she reached for her cup. "You're a lot more fun when you loosen up."

"I'm working. I'm not supposed to be fun."

"Of course. Now, about my passport?"

"Greta should be here any moment."

"Good. There's a plane leaving for Zurich in three hours. I've already changed my reservation."

He rewrapped the turkey sandwich, knowing he wasn't going to eat it. "What about your money? How can you be sure your brother will send it this time?"

"I've already picked it up. Guido was kind enough to stop by the telegraph office on the way here."

"You said your brother was short on money. Do you have enough to get to Switzerland?"

She tossed back her hair, a blush crawling up her neck. "I'm fine."

"I wasn't trying to pry," he said quickly. "I merely wanted to offer to—"

"I said I'm fine."

After a brief knock at the door, it opened, and he tore his concerned gaze away from Gina's stubborn expression in time to see the illusive Greta poke her head inside.

"Shall I come back later?" she asked.

"No," they both said at the same time.

She looked from one to the other as she stepped into the office, a distinct look of amusement lurking in her eyes. Her hands were empty. Not a good sign.

He glanced at Gina. She, too, had clearly noticed that Greta did not come bearing tangible good news.

"I can pay you for my passport now," Gina said, her voice sounding unsure as she reached for her tan leather handbag. She cast another nervous glance at Greta as though waiting for the bomb to drop.

"Hold on to that for a while," Greta said, her tone brisk, businesslike. "I don't actually have your passport yet."

A surge of inexplicable relief astonished Jackson into picking up his pen, then he started to twirl it. Quickly he put it back down.

"Greta," he drawled, satisfied that he sounded suitably impatient.

She lifted one perfectly arched brow at him. "Yes?" she asked with a complete absence of apology.

"This delay is inexcusable."

Gina issued a soft but indelicate snort. "Yeah. What's going on?"

The receptionist's mouth curved in a conciliatory smile. "I'm afraid part of it was my fault. I let the ball drop twice, once after you were feeling ill and I thought you needed time to convalesce, then after you got arrested I figured there was no real rush and we had so many others to—"

Gina speared Jackson with a venomous look. "Did everyone have to know about that?"

He raised his hands in supplication. "She took the original call."

Gina smoothed back her hair and lifted her chin at a haughty angle. "Well, there's no cause for delay now."

"Not on our end," Greta agreed. "But there is that matter of the pending charges against you."

Gina's eyes widened and her helpless gaze flew to Jackson. "But they were false. I thought everything was taken care of."

He shrugged, feeling rather powerless himself. "I should have questioned the officer more thoroughly. I just figured—" He broke off, feeling like an idiot. He'd been too busy being distracted by Gina to do his job properly.

Greta jumped in. "I'm sure it's just a formality to expunge your record. We just have to make sure the matter gets taken care of."

"My record?" Gina echoed, her face blanching briefly before a surge of pink anger blossomed in her cheeks. "This whole thing is nuts. I swear to heaven this will be the last time I set foot in Italy."

On her way to the door, Greta's lips lifted in an irritatingly serene smile. "I'm sure we'll have this cleared up in no time." She paused in the doorway. "Oh, by the way, Mr. Covington, I'm afraid I'm going to have to bow out of the Arabian consulate's dinner tonight."

Jackson groaned. Today was turning out to be no better than yesterday. He never looked forward to this particular annual event. Going solo would make the evening worse. "Are you sure?"

"Sorry," she said, without further explanation. Then her face lit up, barely, but enough to plant a seed of hope in Jackson, and she added, "You could always take Ms. Hart."

Chapter Seven

Gina stared at Ms. Morgan in shocked disbelief. The woman had to be certifiable. Gina was certainly not going anywhere with Jackson, and certainly not to a formal consulate dinner.

And from the look on his face, Jack agreed.

So patently, in fact, it ticked her off. That is, it would have had she cared enough to be ticked off. She didn't. Not in the least. She had no desire to be in his company for one more hour, much less an entire evening.

Gina leaned back against the sofa in a great show of indifference. "Well, Ms. Morgan, I didn't realize you had such a wicked sense of humor."

The other woman smiled indulgently, which served to hurl Gina's irritation up a notch. "It's not a bad idea. Mr. Covington hates going to these functions alone, and it appears you won't have anything to do."

"I'll be getting on a plane for Switzerland," Gina said through gritted teeth. "That's what I'll be doing."

"I rather doubt it," Ms. Morgan said calmly.

Gina glanced at Jackson, wondering what the hell had his tongue so tied. Judging from his expression, he was shocked speechless. Did he find the idea of her being his escort *that* distasteful?

Or was he disappointed that this woman was standing him up?

Gina blinked when comprehension started to dawn, and she remembered her initial impression that Ms. Morgan had the hots for Jack. Maybe it was the other way around, or maybe it was mutual. Funny, Gina hadn't picked up on any particular chemistry between them, but obviously there was enough there that he had asked Greta Morgan for a date. And now she was chumping him.

Gina's position softened. She'd been chumped a couple of times herself. Both times in high school, when in a matter of three weeks she'd sprouted two inches, making her taller than her prom date. His ego had prevented him from going through with their plans. Gina had ended up going to the prom alone.

She sighed to herself. No matter what the reason, or how old you were, being stood up was no fun.

"Even if I am delayed," Gina said, feeling a little more reasonable now, "I wouldn't have anything to wear to a formal dinner."

"Exactly," Jackson finally said, and when Gina's eyes met his, all her charitable thoughts made a dash for the window.

He didn't want her to go. He thought she'd embarrass him. Her temper simmered dangerously close to the surface.

"I'm not going to impose on Ms. Hart just because I find myself having to fly solo this evening," he said, ramming an impatient hand through his hair. "You are forgetting, Ms. Morgan, that Ms. Hart is here as an American citizen in need of our support, which I may point out is sadly lacking."

A brief frown creased the other woman's face as she

stared idly at Jack for a moment, before resting her gaze on Gina. "I think you're about my size." Her thoughtful expression gave way to a wry twist of her pink lips. "In any case, I have a range of two sizes in my closet."

Gina grinned. She couldn't help it. If she'd liked Greta Morgan well enough before, she idolized her now.

"What are you talking about?" Jack asked, his frustration clearly growing.

"Never mind." She glanced at her wristwatch, then made eye contact with Gina again. "I get off work at five-thirty. That should give us enough time."

"Ms. Morgan, I don't think—"

"For goodness' sake, call me Greta. You're practically family," she said, shooting an amused look at Jack's gruff face before she traipsed out the door.

Gina took another sip of her now cold tea, trying to buy enough time to resume normal breathing. When she returned the cup to the saucer, it rudely heralded her haywire nerves with a grating clang only china could make.

What the hell had just happened? she wondered. She should have been on her way to the airport by now. And not having to muster the courage to meet Jack's eyes. He'd lapsed into a sudden and strange silence that did nothing to soothe the parade of raw emotions turning her inside out.

Of course, none of this was her fault. In fact, she was going to write Congress, or whoever was responsible for foreign diplomats, a nasty letter after she got home. She really would. As soon as she found out who her congressman was.

She took a deep breath and forced herself to look at Jack. "Don't worry. I have no intention of going to that dinner with you. Obviously Greta has been working a *little* too hard lately,'' she said with an airy laugh.

He didn't even smile. Steepling his fingers, he leaned back in his chair and stared thoughtfully at her.

After nearly two minutes of his silent perusal, Gina's temper started to ignite. She was the one being inexcusably delayed, who had been falsely arrested, victimized by a thief....

And considered so nonthreatening that Jack's girlfriend was trying to arrange a date for him with her.

The sudden thought stabbed her with a knife of pain so sharp that she abruptly stood, nearly sending the china to the floor. She set the cup and saucer on the coffee table, then smoothed her slacks.

''I guess I'll go get a hotel room,'' she said, anxious to get away from Jack, from the embassy, from people in general. ''I'll call as to where I can be reached once I've settled in. I don't expect my passport can be delayed that much longer. And I should have that matter with the police ironed out by then.''

Her voice and posture were formal. Too formal. Jack had obviously noticed her discomfort. A sympathetic smile curved his lips, and she very much wanted to slap it off his face.

''You don't need to get a hotel room,'' he said. ''You can stay with me.''

''Are you always this accommodating to hapless American tourists?''

She'd either startled or irritated him with her question, if his quick frown was any indication. ''You're the first,'' he said.

''Well, thanks, but no thanks.'' She started for the door.

He stood. "Come on, Gina, be reasonable. You just told me you're short on cash."

But not on dignity. "Actually, I think the embassy ought to pay for my room. It's your screwups causing the delay."

A faint grin made his eyes look suddenly bluer, his face more relaxed. "You have a better shot of getting a free room out of me."

His apparent change in demeanor had her fumbling when she tried to grasp the doorknob. "Yeah, well, you're easy."

He laughed, then let another moment lapse while he stared absently at her. Then his face tensed as though he was having a tough time making a decision. Finally, he said, "Look, dinner won't be so bad. The food will probably be French, the wine smooth and expensive. And the company..." He raised his hand and gestured in a so-so motion. "But I'm sure we'll keep each other entertained."

She leaned a hip against the door and sighed. He got high marks for trying to reassure her. "Jack, can you honestly see me at one of those dinners?"

"Sure," he said, shrugging. "Why not?"

Had there been some hesitation, or had she imagined it? She shook her head. "I wouldn't even know what to talk about."

"Somehow I can't picture you running out of things to say." The lopsided smile he gave her was almost boyish, and so disarming that her heart did a funny little flip.

She couldn't help but smile back. It was a faint one, but enough to steal the conviction from her voice. "It's really a bad idea."

He made a noise of disagreement. "I know you don't have other plans."

"Depends on how long I'm tied up at the police station."

"You let me take care of that," he said, stepping around his desk and moving toward her.

Excitement sizzled in her veins and she stayed, frozen, her hand hovering above the doorknob. Not that she thought he was going to do anything like touch her. Even though he was only a yard away...

Immediately she felt foolish when he walked past her and picked up a magazine off a highly polished corner table. After glancing at it for a few seconds, he held the periodical out to her. "There's an article in here on some of the people who are going to be there tonight. A couple of them will be quite interesting and possibly even entertaining."

So, what was this—homework? Her defenses started to mount again and she firmly gripped the doorknob. "Sorry, they didn't teach us how to read in Brooklyn."

He frowned at her flip remark and, still holding the magazine, let his outstretched hand fall to his side. "If that's supposed to be a joke, I don't get it."

The look he gave her was a combination of bewilderment, uncertainty and suspicion, and it made her feel instantly childish. Maybe she was being too touchy. He *was* urging her to go to the dinner even after she'd given him an easy out.

Oh, God, she hated this. Of course she could fit in with his crowd tonight. She'd been around enough moneyeyed people in the past few years to at least not make a fool of herself. But that he might be the slightest bit unsure stung. Or then again, maybe she was seeing things that weren't there.

She groaned inwardly, loathing even more these internal battles she often waged, going back and forth over the same issue until she knew she was crazier than a New York cab driver.

Man, oh man, she was going to regret this. "Look, if you really want me to go, I will." Her breath seeped out slow and labored as his expression actually lit up. "But I'm not going to borrow a dress from Greta. I'll buy my own."

The sudden thought tumbled out of her mouth before she'd given it any consideration, and now she sucked her breath back in, waiting for his reaction.

"Fine," he said without the slightest hesitation, his face unreadable. "But I insist on paying for it. You're doing me a favor by going."

"No way." She shook her head, adamant. After pausing, and watching him closely, she added, "I'll only buy something I'll wear again, so it's not like you're putting me out."

Still he showed no reaction, even though she was perfectly aware that she'd been trying to goad him into one. "I understand," he said, "but that doesn't mean I can't pay for it. Besides, you are short on cash, remember?"

Okay, so he was willing to trust her taste in choosing a dress. Another point in his favor. She started to relax and admitted to herself that going out with him might be fun. Even though it wasn't officially a date. "True, but I figured you wouldn't mind another IOU."

He smiled, and her heart did that foolish little flip again. "If that's the way you want it," he said, and started to turn back toward his desk.

"Um, I think I'll have a look at that magazine article, after all," she said, irrational excitement beginning to simmer. He'd look terrific in a tuxedo, and for one evening why shouldn't she pretend she was Cinderella?

He handed her the magazine before continuing toward his desk. "I'm going to arrange for a driver to take you to do your shopping," he said, reaching for his phone. "Greta can give you a list of boutiques that carry suitable dresses."

This time Gina's heart sank a little. Still, she ordered herself not to jump to a wrong conclusion. That *was* a practical suggestion, she had to admit. He wasn't necessarily concerned about what she'd choose when left to her own devices.

"I'd appreciate the lift," she said slowly, "but as far as the list of shops, I'm familiar enough with the city. My job has brought me here often enough in the past."

He wanted to argue. That much was clear by the way he furrowed his brow and let his hand weigh with heavy uncertainty on the phone receiver. "Cocktails start at seven. You don't have much time, especially if you require alterations."

She met his eyes directly and held his gaze. "I can handle it."

"I don't like being late."

She smiled a little then. "I bet you've never been late a day in your life."

"Some people consider that a virtue."

"Count me as one of them," she said with sincerity, in spite of her own not-so-reliable track record. "I won't let you ruin your standing."

He stared at her a moment longer, silently, assessingly. "Go get your dress, Gina."

Without breaking eye contact, she reached for the doorknob. "Anything else I need to know?"

Jack hesitated. "One last thing."

Here it came. The pointed but benign lecture on no short, tight skirts, no plunging necklines, no sleazy dresses...as if she wasn't savvy enough to know better.

"I know you're already aware of this," he started, and she braced herself, resigned, and just a little disappointed. "Siesta begins in another hour and the shops will be closed for a while. You might want to get started right away."

JACKSON INSPECTED his bow tie using the antique oak mirror hanging in his apartment's foyer while he waited for Gina. Per his suggestion, she'd moved back into the room she'd slept in last night, and he hadn't seen so much as a glimpse of her since he'd come home an hour ago.

Isabella knew him well, and he must have looked anxious because she'd assured him twice now that his guest was almost ready. His housekeeper was Gina's newest fan.

His gaze strayed to the large bouquet of pink and white flowers sitting on the foyer table, waiting to be taken home by Isabella. Gina had bought them for the older woman, as a thank you, his housekeeper had told him, her eyes lighting up with pleasure even then, over the explanation of the small kindness.

As much as he admired Gina's thoughtfulness, he'd been irritated, too. More, he'd been ashamed. He should have been the one who had inspired that kind of delight in his deserving housekeeper's face. But the truth was, he never thought of little things like flowers.

He'd immediately pulled the leather-bound book out of his jacket pocket and made a note to order an arrangement for Marcy tomorrow. And then he added Greta's name to his list. And finally Gina's.

She was included, of course, because she was doing him a favor tonight. That she would be thrilled and excited and her brown eyes would probably light up and sparkle like a Christmas tree had nothing to do with his decision. Nothing at all.

He glanced at his watch as he returned the notebook to his pocket. Leaving right now would be the only way they could possibly make it to the cocktail reception before dinner. So much for Gina's assurances.

Staring at the reflection of his bow tie again, he adjusted the dipping right side and wondered about what she had elected to wear. He'd be a liar if he didn't admit to a twinge or two of misgiving over not insisting that Greta help her find something suitable. He found Gina's tastes in clothes a little too trendy, and he didn't want her to feel out of place at the dinner.

He yanked the bow tie free and started retying it. Who the hell was he kidding? He'd been thinking about himself this afternoon when he'd subtly tried to manipulate Gina into accepting Greta's help. He hadn't wanted her to show up in something totally inappropriate and make him look like a jerk. Hell, apparently he didn't need her help. He was doing a good enough job of being an ass all by himself.

Although he had earlier considered bribing Isabella for a hint as to what Gina was going to wear, he'd quickly quashed the idea. She was going to look great. No doubt she'd charm the entire Arabian delegation. Just like she'd enchanted everyone else.

"I'm ready," she said, her voice husky, slightly breathless, coming from behind him, and sweetening the air like a cloud of whipped cream.

His eyes caught hers in the mirror, and they were bright and sparkly and just a little anxious as she peered back at him. He winked, and fine, crinkly smile lines promptly fanned out from her lashes, her pink-tinted lips curving up toward them. He could see nothing below her chin, and not wanting to appear too solicitous, he made a final adjustment to his tie before turning around.

"I'm not late, am I?" she asked. "Isabella told me I had until six-thirty."

He didn't bother pointing out that it was nearly six-forty. He was too damned relieved with what he saw. Still feeling a little like a jerk, but damned relieved, too.

She looked beautiful, if a little strained, and amazingly conservative. The black dress she wore started under her chin and the hem skimmed her ankles. "You're right on time," he said, and held out an arm to her.

She didn't move, but let her arms hang loosely at her sides, her smile drooping to nonexistence. "You don't like the dress."

Surprised, Jackson frowned and let his own arm drop. At least the relief hadn't shown. "Why would you say that? It's a perfectly charming dress."

She shook her head, her fingers fluttering to the high black satin neck band. The armholes were deeply cut, showing off slightly tanned, well-toned arms, but that was the only skin showing. "I can tell by the look on your face that you don't care for it." When he started to protest, she held up a silencing hand. "And that's okay. Obviously our tastes differ, but I want to know if you think it's appropriate for tonight."

It was. No question about it. But he didn't offer that opinion right away, because if he didn't appear to at least give the matter some thought, she would probably still argue.

So instead, he furrowed his eyebrows in greatly exaggerated concentration and gave her the once-over. She sighed, clearly exasperated, and he laughed, although she was right. He wasn't crazy about the dress. He'd have preferred to see a little more skin, definitely a lot more leg. But he couldn't fault her choice: black, understated and entirely appropriate for a consulate dinner.

"Well?" she said, with more than a hint of impatience.

He turned up a palm. "What can I say? You look beautiful."

She cocked her head to the side and gazed at him with mild rebuke.

"I'm being perfectly honest," he said. "You look incredible."

She didn't believe him. The annoyed twist of her mouth told him that, and made her unexpectedly endearing. This was a different side to Gina—vulnerable, concerned about fitting in. He didn't want her to worry. He hadn't lied. She looked stunning.

Ignoring the compliment, she slid her gaze to his bow tie. She squinted slightly at it, then a small grin tugged at one corner of her mouth. "Need help with that?"

"Think you could do better?" Doubtless she could. For some reason, he always had trouble with bow ties.

She stepped toward him and her mysterious feminine scent sucker punched him, sending him off balance, making him want to call off the entire evening.

Not the entire evening. What suddenly popped into his mind did not involve a roomful of foreign dignitaries.

He shifted back, the action automatic yet subtle, and she briefly gazed up at him, curiosity and wariness doing provocative things to her brown eyes. She reached out long, supple fingers that brushed his jaw, lightly scraped his chin, and when her gaze slipped to his mouth, he knew if he kissed her, she wouldn't resist.

"*Fretta, fretta.* You will be late, *signore.*"

Coming from the kitchen, Isabella's words warned them a second before she appeared.

"There," Gina said, quickly stepping back, her gaze lowered, ostensibly to inspect her handiwork. "Much better."

He wanted to catch her eye. She was wise to avoid him. In fact, he thought, willing his tightened body to settle down, the conservative dress was probably a good choice, after all. Maybe it wasn't even conservative enough. She had far too many curves for any dress to disguise.

Isabella made a shooing gesture with her hands. "Go. Go. You hate to be late, Signore Covington."

He motioned for Gina to precede him. When she started toward the door, a flash of leg caught his attention and he noticed the long slit that ended about mid-thigh. The effect was subtle yet sexy, and hit him like a two-by-four.

He wondered what happened when she sat down.

Suddenly realizing that he looked like a damn smitten twelve-year-old, he quickly raised his gaze.

His heart slammed its next beat. Shock knotted in his chest and blocked air passage to his lungs.

The dress had no back.

Tanned skin, framed into a diamond shape and trimmed with black satin, was exposed from her nape and down to the top of her buttocks. Her back was smooth, silky looking, without any distracting bathing suit marks, and it made his palms itch like they had no right to.

Following her out the door, he removed a handkerchief from his pocket and wiped his brow. This was going to be a very long night.

ose him, and it made her pulse pound and her pain
to rise.

Following her out the door, he snatched a handkerchief from his pocket and wiped his brow. This was
going to be a very long night.

Chapter Eight

By the time they had been served their first glass of
champagne, Gina had pretty much decided the dress had
probably backfired. She didn't know who was more nervous, her or Jackson.

After downing the bubbly appallingly quickly, she
traded in her empty crystal flute for one filled with min-
eral water. Jackson was too busy schmoozing with the
assistant French consul to notice, and she was grateful.
She didn't want him to know how much his smoldering
looks had unsettled her. Although she doubted he even
realized how he was looking at her. Which proved to
be her only small consolation. If he did, her guess was
he'd be dumbfounded.

She smiled with gleeful relish at the thought, and a
young blond man standing near the reception line, mistaking her private joke, smiled back and started to ap-
proach her.

Oh, great.

As nonchalantly as she could, she shifted and slipped
an arm through Jack's. His startled gaze turned to sweep
her face just as the other man stopped in front of them.

Jack's eyes reluctantly left hers to rest on the younger

man's thin face. He nodded to him and said something in French.

Her high school French more than a little rusty, the only thing Gina gleaned from the interchange was that the man's name was Henri.

After shaking hands with Jack, he glanced at Gina and said in heavily accented English, "Your companion? She is American?"

Jack's mouth curved, but it wasn't a smile she was used to, and somehow she knew he didn't particularly care for this man. "Yes," he said, amicably enough, "This is Gina Hart. Gina, this is Henri La Fontaine. He is one of the French ambassador's assistants."

"Then we must speak English." Henri picked up her free hand, made a point of meeting her eyes, then said, *"Enchanté,"* before bowing to brush his lips across her skin.

Gina took an instant dislike to him and wanted to wipe off the faint moisture his sloppy, unwelcome kiss left. "A pleasure to meet you, Monsieur La Fontaine," she said, and knew her smile was too tight. She took a quick, deep breath. She could be cordial for Jack's sake.

"Please. You must call me Henri." His green eyes were red-rimmed, and she suspected he didn't need the champagne refill for which he signaled the waiter. "May I have your glass refreshed?" he asked.

"I'm fine. Thank you." She glanced at Jack and started to pull her arm away. "If you'll excuse me, I think I'll duck into the ladies' room."

He pressed his arm against his side, momentarily trapping her hand. He gave it a quick squeeze. "Do you know where it is?"

"I would be most happy to escort you," Henri offered, taking a fresh glass of champagne off the tray without so much as a glance of acknowledgment at the waiter.

"Thanks, La Fontaine, but I'll show her. Nice seeing you." Jack cupped her elbow and gently spun her away from the man's unnerving gaze, and judging by the look on Henri's face, he was equally as surprised as she was by Jack's abruptness.

"I didn't mean to interrupt you," she mumbled. "In fact, I was trying to bow out so you could have a private discussion if you wanted."

He slid her an amused look that bordered annoyingly on cynical. "Trust me. I'm not the one whose attention he wanted."

What did he think? That she'd invited the guy's leers? She shook away from his hold, but a second later she felt his hand at her back. Her bare back.

The fact that his skin was suddenly touching hers apparently gave him pause, too, because his fingers stiffened. As much as she wished he would, he didn't pull away. Instead, his hand started to relax and his warm palm molded her lower spine, the ends of his fingers stretching to caress the indentation of her waist.

Goose bumps sprang to the surface of her flesh in mortifying speed, down her bare arms, across her exposed back.

She gritted her teeth and used all her willpower to keep her face aimed straight ahead, but she couldn't help sweeping his somber profile with a quick sidelong glance. Slowly, amusement tugged at the corner of his mouth visible to her. Damn him.

She stopped, breaking contact as she turned to face him. "You don't have to baby-sit me. Go ahead and mingle, or whatever. I promise to catch up to you by the time they ring the dinner chimes."

He frowned. "How do you know about the dinner chimes?"

She lifted her chin. "I'm not as ignorant as you think."

"I never said that," he protested, looking truly offended.

"Chill out, Jackson, that was just a figure of speech." She shrugged. "It was a guess. I've been to other formal dinners where a waiter walks around ringing a bell or the orchestra plays a certain song that signals dinner. Or they ring chimes." She glanced around at the ornately carved spiral staircase, the etched gold wall sconces and original oil paintings gracing the flocked wallpaper, the crystal chandeliers that probably dated back a hundred years. "I figured this was a chime-ringing kind of place."

He chuckled. "I guess you could put it that way."

"Go be with your friends, Jackson. Don't worry about me." She started to turn away, but he touched her arm, his hand warm and caressing, and she froze as though he held a gun to her head.

"I wouldn't call these people my friends. But I do have to be sociable and mingle. Being here is part of my job."

"I know. I told you to go do that, didn't I?"

At her sharp tone, he frowned. "Has someone upset you? Or do you feel like I've neglected you in any way?"

She waved a dismissive hand. "No, I didn't mean to be short with you. I just don't—" She sighed, staring off across the room at the sea of tuxedoes and elegant cocktail gowns.

Granted, her dress wasn't the least conservative one here, but she was definitely in a minuscule minority. In fact, the only other one that rivaled hers in daring to push the envelope was a low-cut red number worn by a bleach-blonde with dark roots, who looked no more like she belonged here than Gina did.

She'd caught the startled glances when people got a load of the back of her dress, and she felt bad. Her poor judgment was a reflection on Jackson. And he didn't deserve this.

Once again she thought about the smoldering looks he'd given her earlier when she'd tried to seek reassurance. Now she realized that it was entirely possible the long, heated glances were based on murderous intent.

She brought her gaze back to his probing one.

"You were saying?" he prompted.

She stared back, pursing her lips, while thinking about what she wanted to say. Should she apologize? Offer to leave? Henri had not been the first man to come on to her tonight, and although the passes had been subtle, she didn't want to court trouble.

Then again, maybe she was overreacting because she felt out of place. Jack hadn't given her any indication he was displeased with her.

"Look, Gina, I don't think it's any secret that I'm ambitious, that some day I want to be the consul general, just like my father was, and his father before him. These dinners are important to me, and if I seem distracted, I apologize, but it is business. Maybe I didn't explain this well enough when I asked you to come. I apologize for that, too."

Gina stared at him. She was such an idiot...an inconsiderate, self-righteous idiot. Of course this was business for him, and who was she to interfere with his reputation in the tiniest way? "You probably won't believe me, but I wasn't trying to sabotage you with this dress," she said, miserable, and feeling suddenly very tired. "I mean, sure I felt a little smug because it's a little deceiving, but that was only because I couldn't find another dress in time. I'm so tall that—"

He grabbed her upper arms, and when that garnered the attention of several curious people, he released her, one hand trailing her arm until their hands connected, and he pulled her toward a long hall.

They ended up near the ladies' powder room after all, and although they weren't afforded complete privacy, the area was far more removed than the middle of the foyer would have been.

Before he opened his mouth, she said, "I can catch a cab home. There's no need for you to leave and screw up dinner."

"Look, Gina, I don't know why you're being so hard on yourself, but I'm glad you came with me. I *like* the dress. You look beautiful. How many more ways do I have to tell you that?"

Oh, God, now he thought she was fishing for compliments. "Yeah, but..."

He stunned her by pressing the pad of his thumb to her lips. The rest of his hand splayed her jaw. "No yeah-buts."

His head had bent closer, and the wild thought that he might kiss her made her pulse lap twice around the track. As a test, she allowed her lips to soften.

He blinked, a fleeting expression of surprise crossing his face, and he dropped his hand.

She took a shaky breath. "But you want to be consul general, and this is not a consul general's dress."

She startled a laugh out of him. "No problem. I have no intention of borrowing it."

Gina made a face. "You know what I mean."

"Relax," he said, bringing a hand up to her left shoulder, then starting to massage the knot of tension he found. "I'm not consul general yet."

In spite of her anxiety, she let her eyes drift closed. He had great hands...magic hands.

"Quit looking like that," he said, his voice suddenly gruff, and before she could lift her lashes, he'd dropped his hand. "Or you're right, I'll either end up arrested, or the embassy's janitor."

It took her a second to refocus. "Huh?"

"Never mind. Let's go rub elbows. I promise not to neglect you."

After that brief massage, she wanted to rub more than his elbow. "Uh, sure, but I won't be offended if you want me to—" She started to hike a thumb over her shoulder toward the door, but he caught her hand in his and made a fist around it.

"Come on, Gina," he said, pulling her gently back toward the ballroom. "Put on your happy face."

She meekly followed, feeling far more reassured that he didn't hate the dress...or her. In fact, unless she was totally out in left field, she was receiving a different sort of vibe from him altogether. One that had her heart pounding faster than a woodpecker in full swing.

It didn't escape her notice that as soon as they moved closer to the crowd he dropped her hand. But that didn't bother her. Much. This wasn't supposed to be a date.

Thankfully, within ten minutes, the dinner chimes saved them both from any more small talk. Once she'd relaxed, Gina started enjoying listening to all the different foreign languages and accents, and checking out those dignitaries who wore their national dress. The women tended to do so far more than the men, reminding Gina that for all the strides of women's lib, it was still a man's world, especially here in this international sphere of diplomatic envoys and government attachés. For the most part, men made the decisions. Women were their hood ornaments.

The thought was oddly depressing, although she couldn't fathom why, since her uneasiness went beyond basic indignation on behalf of women in general. This wasn't her world. After tonight, she didn't have to give this strange yet privileged way of life a second thought.

Three long tables were set in the main dining room, easily seating twenty people each and boasting a breath-taking array of fine crystal and gleaming gold-trimmed china. Not one hint of a smudge marred the highly pol-ished silver serving trays and utensils. And large clus-ters of exotic fresh flowers were so artfully arranged that they appeared to have sprung from the tables them-selves.

Having allowed some distance to drift between her and Jack as they entered the dining room, Gina was the first to spot the burgundy china place card scripted with Jack's name in gold. She got a little nervous when she didn't see her name right away, then ordered herself to calm down. She had been a last-minute invite, after all.

Still, all the place settings were assigned, which meant there was either no place for her or their host had split up the couples. She made a frantic motion with her eyes to get Jack's attention. He saw her, passed a hovering waiter his nearly empty champagne glass and strode toward her.

In spite of her alarm, she liked watching his easy grace, the self-assured way he interacted with others, the confident way he held himself. She liked the way he smiled at her.

"Did you find our places?" he asked, his sultry

breath tickling her ear, and she had to remind herself that this was not the time to get all hot and bothered.

"Sort of. You're right there." She started to point, figured that would be rude, so nodded toward his place card. "I can't find me."

His eyebrows drew together, his gaze darting to the place setting on his left. Irritation flashed in his eyes. "You're right beside me. They made a mistake."

She squinted at the name scripted in gold. "Are you sure? Who's Miranda? What if she comes looking for her place?"

"She won't." He leaned over and turned the place card so that the name side rested against the white lace tablecloth.

"But what if she—"

He pulled out her chair. "Gina, sit down."

Ordinarily it would have annoyed her to be ordered around like that, but he sounded more weary than bossy, so she took her seat, but not without sliding him a quizzical look, which he pointedly ignored.

Before seating himself, he pulled out the other chair to his right and waited until the older woman with the bluish French twist had positioned herself to her liking.

Only half the guests from the other tables were already seated, but within minutes everyone else had taken their places and the white-gloved waiters were beginning to pour the wine and serve the first course.

Gina was still curious as to how Jack knew that the Miranda person wasn't going to be here, but the blue-haired woman had obviously taken a liking to him and had monopolized his attention from the time they sat down.

After mentally doing her no-fail chant, Gina picked up the seafood fork in order to attack the plump broiled scallops in lime butter they had just been served. The assortment of silverware from which to choose was dizzying, and even though she was confident she'd made the right choice, she couldn't help but sneak a peek at the people on her left to double-check herself.

Sitting several seats away was the bleach-blonde… and an avalanche of cleavage. The woman met her gaze, and her red-tinted lips curved in a timid smile. Gina blinked. Was it coincidence, or was this the bimbo section? The uncharitable thought popped into her head before she could stop it, and brief, irrational anger stole her appetite.

She was, of course, including herself, which was what hurt so much. Although, her conclusion was undoubtedly absurd. Whoever had arranged their seating didn't know her, didn't know she'd be wearing this dress. In fact, the seat had been reserved for someone named Miranda.

"Something wrong with the scallops?" Jack asked quietly.

She started at the nearness of his voice, then realized she'd been holding her fork in midair while thinking like a silly, insecure twit.

Sighing, she shook her head, then set aside the fork and picked up her wineglass. This wasn't like her. Not the new her, anyway. She'd left those insecurities behind about six years ago, and she wasn't at all keen on reverting to old form.

It helped little that she knew what the problem was. He was sitting beside her. She wanted too much for Jack to like her, and she hated herself for allowing this vulnerability to make her feel raw, needy and irrational. She would be leaving Rome soon. She doubted she'd even see Jack again after tomorrow.

The idea stung, and when her eyes met his again, she admitted to herself that she wanted very much to be his friend. Maybe even more.

She forced a smile. "Why haven't you started eating? Can't figure out which fork to use?"

He laughed out loud, startling her and several of their closer dinner companions.

"You certainly are in good spirits tonight, Jackson," the balding man across the table from them said, a faint smile lifting his ruddy bulldog cheeks. He slid a pointed look at Gina. "Aren't you going to introduce us to your lovely companion?"

"Forgive me." Looking momentarily chagrined, Jackson put a hand at the back of Gina's chair and glanced at her, his blue gaze full of apology. "This is Gina Hart from New York."

She smiled, wishing all eyes were not suddenly on her. But she managed to maintain the smile as Jack introduced the Irish ambassador's assistant and his wife, two attachés from Arabia, a French diplomat with a title she didn't recognize, as well as several other emissaries from the Italian and Swiss governments. Her head started to ache by the final round of introductions, but not so much that she didn't notice the blonde was the only person Jack didn't seem to already know. A fact that didn't surprise Gina one bit, although it did cause her mild irritation.

The blonde's companion, an Italian attaché, was the last to be presented to Gina, and after a brief pause, he took his cue and introduced his companion, who turned out to be his fiancée.

If the rest of the guests were as surprised as Gina, they hid their reactions well. All except for the blue-haired woman who ended up being the recent widow of some French big shot. She immediately turned to her neighbor and began talking in a dismissive gesture that remained a hair short of rude. Everyone else offered congratulations to the couple, their well-bred manners keeping polite smiles on their tolerant faces.

Gina picked up her fork again and hoped she wasn't expected to remember names. Apart from the daunting amount of information she'd just been given, she admittedly had been distracted from trying to absorb all the difficult foreign names and titles. Her focus had been on the women's dresses. Black, most of them, high-necked, in general, and all carrying a bounty higher than the salary of three of her courier jobs combined.

Good thing this wasn't a competition, she reminded herself, the chip forming on her shoulder threatening to set her off balance. She slid a furtive glance at the blonde—Brigitte. Gina remembered her name, probably because the woman didn't look like a Brigitte. Taffy would have been more appropriate, or Bambi, maybe.

"So, Ms. Hart, do you work for the American embassy?"

The Irish ambassador's assistant's question took her by surprise, and she started, guiltily, her fork clanging against the china plate. She deserved this, she figured, for sitting here in judgment of poor Brigitte, who looked as clueless as Gina.

"No," she said, smiling, "I'm just here for a few days."

"On holiday?"

She fought to keep her smile intact. What was with this guy?

She exhaled slowly. Nothing. Absolutely nothing. He

was merely making conversation. She was just being touchy.

"A combination of business and pleasure." She speared a scallop, hoping the guy would get the hint and shut up. She wasn't sure what Jack wanted her to say. It was doubtful he'd be happy with her admitting that he'd picked up a flaky American tourist, without enough sense not to get pickpocketed...or arrested.

"Oh?" The man smiled with interest. "And what kind of business are you in?"

Gina abandoned the scallop without so much as a nibble and wondered how much trouble she'd be asking for by claiming to be an international attorney, or maybe a museum curator. Hell, even an art thief sounded better than a glorified gofer.

Damn it. She liked being a courier. It was fun and exciting, and the opportunity exposed her to interesting cultures she'd hardly have experienced in Brooklyn. She'd never been ashamed of her chosen profession before, and she wasn't going to be now. Not even for Jack's sake.

She took a deep breath, about to answer, when Jack said, "Gina is a courier. She carries packages between the United States and Europe."

"Actually, I go to Asia and South America, too," Gina said, her gaze briefly lingering with curiosity on Jack's face. Not only had he not hesitated to reveal her occupation, but he hadn't seemed the least bit put off by its lack of sophistication.

"For the embassy?" the woman in the cream-and-black velvet dress across from her asked.

Gina made a slightly sheepish face. "The highest bidder usually gets my attention."

The man beside her laughed. "That's what I like,"

he said in a booming voice and a German accent. "Good sound American capitalism."

Several other people laughed along with him, and Gina slanted Jack a glance, hoping he was equally amused.

He gave her a private wink that made her insides melt faster than warmed butter, then bowed his head close to hers. "I think Diana Frost is trying to get your attention again. She's the one in the black velvet dress. Her husband is on her right—Jonathan Frost."

Gina nodded her appreciation, then directed her gaze toward Diana Frost.

The woman leaned forward, excitement heightening the color in her pale cheeks. "Ms. Hart, I would really like to talk to you about this courier job of yours later if you wouldn't mind. I've been encouraging my daughter to do something like that."

"Call me Gina, please. And I'd be happy to discuss it with you." She breathed a sigh of relief. Apparently no one thought she was a flake. In fact, most everyone else had gone on to chat about other things. And bless Diana Frost. She was actually interested in what Gina did.

"After dinner, then?" The woman glanced at Jack, then back to Gina. "I assume you're staying for dancing?"

"Dancing?" Gina echoed, her voice a faint, horrified whisper.

"Of course," Jack said. "We wouldn't miss it."

Chapter Nine

Just when Gina thought she could enjoy her dinner after all, dread coated her mouth and drowned her taste buds. She was not going to dance. She was not even going to pretend to tap her foot in time with the music, period.

She chewed one of the tasteless scallops, swallowed it, then stuck another one in her mouth and swept a glance at everyone else's plate. Most of her dinner companions were finished. Gina's plate was nearly full, no matter how much she'd tried to spread the scallops around. Briefly she thought about ditching a couple of the little suckers under the table, but that would be childish.

"Don't you like your food?" Jack whispered close to her ear.

"I don't dance," she whispered back.

"Ah, so that's the problem."

She didn't have to look at him to know he was smiling. She could hear the amusement in his voice. Well, he himself had said she was doing him a favor. She would simply insist they leave after dinner.

"No problem," she denied sweetly, then set down her fork when she saw that the waiters had started to clear away the plates.

"Why don't you dance?" Jack leaned back and stretched an arm across the back of her chair, bringing his mouth so close to her ear her pulse picked up speed.

"I just never learned." She gazed around the table, looking for a distraction. But everyone seemed to be engaged in a conversation with the person beside them. Except the blonde. Brigitte fidgeted nervously with her napkin, eyes downcast, while her fiancé laughed with the woman on his left.

Gina felt sorry for Brigitte, but she wasn't sure how she could include her. Nor if she really wanted to.

"It's not hard," Jack said. "A few turns around the floor tonight and you'll be a pro."

Her gaze skidded to his. "I'm not dancing."

He frowned, his face close, and she found herself angling subtly away. "All right."

He didn't understand, and she didn't want to explain it to him. Especially not when he was so close, looking so bewildered and at such a loss at her sharp tone.

She sighed. "Look, when I was in high school, I was taller than every guy in my class, and when it came time for dances... Well, it just didn't work out, that's all."

"It's been a long time since high school—"

"Not *that* long."

He smiled indulgently. "I'm a good four inches taller than you are, *and* I'm a great teacher."

"If you think I'm going out there and have you teach me in front of everyone, you're nuts." In her excitement, her voice had risen slightly, so she glanced around to make sure she hadn't been overheard.

No one seemed to be paying them any attention. Except Brigitte. But it was clear she hadn't heard. She simply looked a little lost.

Gina leaned back in her chair to give the waiter room to serve the soup, and glared at Jack at the same time, giving him a silent signal that their discussion was over.

"You'll change your mind once the music starts," he said.

"Wanna bet?"

He gave her another one of those indulgent smiles that was beginning to grate on her nerves.

Everyone else was served their soup, and then dinner progressed through five additional courses over the next two hours. Gina had to stifle several yawns before coffee and dessert were finally served. A different wine had accompanied each course, and although she'd been careful to take only a couple of sips of each glass, she was still terribly sleep-deprived and felt slightly mellow as a result.

After all the plates were cleared away, the guest of honor, a visiting dignitary from the Arabian government, rose to say a few words while cognac was being sipped and expensive cigars lit.

Gina inconspicuously covered her mouth with her hand and struggled valiantly against a threatening yawn.

Jack saw it. He ran his arm along the back of her chair and gave her shoulder a gentle squeeze. "It's almost over," he whispered.

As if on cue, applause broke out among the dinner guests. Then, as the fanfare wound down, music, drifting in from the ballroom, immediately replaced it.

Several of the men pushed back their chairs, Jack included. He presented her his hand, and she placed her palm on his and allowed him to help her up. The brief contact made her already fuzzy head a little blurrier. Of course, she knew it wasn't his touch that caused the sensation. It was the wine, too much rich food....

"This doesn't mean I'm dancing," she said once she stood.

"I understand." He placed his hand at the small of her back and guided her toward the music.

If his previous touch had made her a little light-headed, his warm palm pressed to her bare skin made her feel positively faint. Except she knew she wouldn't do anything so foolish as to keel over. She wanted the feeling to last.

She leaned toward him, absorbing his strength, until their bodies met in some interesting places. Her forwardness shocked her, but when he didn't resist, she stayed where she was as they strolled toward the ballroom.

Several couples had already taken to the floor, the women's chiffon skirts swirling across the polished parquet floor, and sequined bodices glittering beneath the sparkling chandeliers.

Suddenly Gina wished she did know how to dance. She wanted to be part of the fairy tale and not just watch it unfold from the sidelines. More important, she wanted to give Jack a reason to hold her.

Unconsciously she'd pressed even closer to him while she watched the couples glide effortlessly across the floor. His breath stirred her hair, his palm branded her flesh.

"We'd be better off out there," he said, his mouth close when she tilted her head back to look quizzically at him. But he offered no further explanation. He didn't have to. The desire in his eyes, the heat emanating from his body said it all.

She pulled away, self-conscious suddenly, and used a shaky hand to smooth the line of her dress. A quick glance around told her that no one had appeared to notice how cozy they had been.

Jack smiled at her transparent expression, then his face sobered and his attention drifted to a spot over her shoulder. "Looks like we're about to have company."

She followed his gaze and was dismayed to find Henri La Fontaine approaching them. She wasn't sure why she'd taken such an instant dislike to the man. He hadn't overtly offended her in any way, but upon seeing him, an unwelcome feeling of unease crawled over her like ants at a picnic.

"Maybe we should try one dance," she said. "But we stay in the corner. And don't move your feet too much."

"Yes, ma'am. I would love to have this dance," he said with a mock bow and a lift of one eyebrow. "Even if it is by default."

"Come on, Jackson," she said, grabbing his hand and glancing furtively at Henri, "before the damn song is over."

"You have such a way with words," he said, amusement lacing his voice as she grabbed his hand and led him onto the crowded floor.

"Yeah, wait till you see what my feet can do."

Weaving in and out of couples who were all too well coordinated for her peace of mind, she guided them as close to a corner as possible, then turned to face him.

He was looking at her, an odd expression of expectation on his face.

"What?" She squinted up at him. "I did something wrong already, didn't I?"

His initial response was a long, nerve-racking moment of silence as he studied her face, brushed a lock of hair off her flushed cheek. Then he said, "Have I told you how much I like this dress?"

His arm slipped around her waist, drawing her closer, and she was astonished to feel how tight his body had become. The discovery shocked her, made her fumble. He tightened his hold.

She caught her breath. Maybe his cummerbund had slipped, maybe his fly had somehow bunched. Maybe… his…his…

Heaven help her. Surely she couldn't be feeling what she thought she was feeling.

She tilted her head back to look at him, her hips shifting slightly away at the same time. "Actually, you said otherwise earlier."

"I'm sure you're mistaken."

As she stared directly into his eyes, she knew she wasn't mistaken. On either count. A primal longing deepened the blue of his eyes to the color of midnight, mesmerizing her with its intensity, weakening her with its blatant yearning.

But this wasn't the time or place. And sadly, Jackson wasn't the right man. He wanted to be consul general, and she still wore eau de Brooklyn. No, he wasn't the right man for her at all. He'd break her heart.

She blinked, and the glitter and sparkle of the other women's gowns caught her eye, reminding her that this was a fairy tale. One that could have a bearable ending only if she remembered she was no Cinderella.

"THIS CAN'T BE HAPPENING." Gina paced Jackson's office, repeatedly jamming her hands through her hair and muttering to herself.

He resisted the urge to pick up his pen and start flipping it around again, yesterday's disastrous results still fresh in his mind. But like her, he was frustrated. Maybe for different reasons, but frustrated nevertheless.

"I can't believe the police insist on holding me here in Italy. Those charges are absurd and they know it." She sighed loudly before collapsing on his couch, clearly exhausted by her frantic pacing. "It's even more difficult to believe that you guys can't do anything about it."

She was going to have to do something about her hair. As attractive as it was all sexy and tousled, he didn't want her leaving his office looking this way. The staff was starting to talk. Not that he'd actually heard any of the rumors, but after two days of Gina being almost a permanent fixture behind his closed door, and him getting absolutely zero work done, tongues were bound to wag.

Especially when she looked like this—eyes bright, sparkling, her hair shining, her mouth moist and...

Her accusing eyes met his. "What are you looking at?"

He straightened and assumed his no-nonsense consulate face. "Don't go pointing fingers. The solicitation charges would have been easy enough to have dismissed if you hadn't tried to buy a black market passport."

Her mouth dropped open, then after an astonished silence she let out a loud shriek.

He cringed, glanced at his closed door, briefly wondered what kind of field day the secretarial pool would have with that outburst, then put up a hand, pleading for her patience.

"I know you did no such thing," he said in a soothing voice. "I only meant that if you hadn't since been *accused* of the black market passport incident, then matters would be simpler.''

''That's not what you said.'' Her lips got plump and pouty and so damn kissable, he thought seriously about irritating her again. ''You said—''

''I know what I said. It was wrong. I apologize.'' He reached for his phone. ''Bickering isn't going to get us any place. Let's see if Greta has found out anything yet.''

''This is so absurd. Why would I try to buy a black market passport when I thought you would have one for me at any minute? Besides that, I didn't have any money to buy one even if I wanted to. Stupid. Really, really stupid.'' Shaking her head, she kept muttering about the ineptness of the Italian police while he waited for his call to connect.

He'd already heard her argument...several times, in fact, but he let her mumble on, hoping she'd get it out of her system. Wisely, he didn't point out that having no money for the passport wasn't viable reasoning. According to Greta, the police alleged Gina had been willing to trade a few favors for the illegal passport. But he decided Gina was in no mood to hear that particular detail.

Besides, they'd have the misunderstanding cleared up in no time. Then Gina could be on her way to Switzerland.

And he'd miss her.

The startling realization stuck in his throat like a square peg in a round hole, and when Greta's relief answered the phone he was barely able to croak out a greeting.

After barking instructions for Greta to call him as

soon as she returned, he replaced the receiver and found Gina watching him with wary hostility.

She folded her arms across her chest, her shirt tightening in a place at which he had no business staring. "Way to win friends and influence people, Bucko."

"Damn it. Greta is starting to annoy the hell out of me." He stopped. "Bucko? First it was Jack and now Bucko. Is Jackson too difficult for you to remember?"

Incredibly, Gina Hart looked sheepish. But only for one blessed moment. "I remembered to call you Jackson the entire night, didn't I?"

He picked up his pen and allowed himself one small twirl. Finally, she'd brought up last night. He'd started to think the entire evening had been a hallucination. A very pleasant one.

He cleared his throat. "You were an excellent companion last night. I'm sorry I didn't mention it sooner. But I really appreciated your company."

She sniffed. "I wasn't looking for thanks. I had fun."

He chuckled.

"I did." At her insistence, her chin lifted in that small, indignant pose he'd come to recognize.

"Careful," he said, "or I may drag you to another dinner tonight." He watched her closely, waiting for a reaction. Not that he knew what response he expected, or hoped for...or even dreaded.

But when a small, enthusiastic smile flashed, albeit faintly, before it disappeared, satisfaction surged in his chest.

"Sorry, but I'll be on my way to Switzerland," she said, starting to ram her fingers though her hair again. "Right?"

He picked up the phone and pressed a button. "Marcy? Have you seen Greta this morning?"

Pinching the bridge of his nose, he closed his eyes against the bright sunlight streaming in his window while he listened to his secretary spout the wrong answer. Another sleepless night and he was going to have to start getting attitude adjustments before he inflicted himself on his staff each morning.

Although he suspected that as soon as Gina left, and the soft sounds of her padding from the guest room to the bathroom as she readied herself for bed stopped, he'd be visiting dreamland again. Her low, throaty humming was something else that got to him. He didn't know how humming could sound so sensual, but she managed to send his thoughts haywire every time she purred an old Bob Seger song under her breath when she thought no one was listening.

After asking Marcy to locate Greta, he managed to hang up the phone without broadcasting his escalating temper.

"I see you have a lot of pull around here." Gina leaned back against the sofa, her short skirt showing enough leg to goad him without her barbed jabs.

He exhaled, wanting to laugh at the irony. Usually he did have a lot of pull. But ever since Gina Hart had stepped on embassy soil, everything had gone to hell. Including his ability to concentrate. And that unfortunate slip was not going to place him in line for the retiring consul general's position.

He stared at her for a long, intense minute, hoping to disconcert the annoying smugness out of her.

She blinked. It was a start.

"What is up with you?" he asked, his voice calm, reasonable. "I thought you had a nice time last night."

Her eyes widened, briefly, before they narrowed. "I did."

"So why the attitude this morning? And why do I get the feeling I've done something wrong?"

"No." Her denial was swift, her eyes turning wary again. "You didn't do anything wrong. Everything was..." She rose from the sofa and walked over to gaze out the window. "Dinner was a lot more pleasant than I thought it would be."

He half laughed. "I guess I painted too bleak a picture. I'm probably jaded from attending too many of these functions."

She swiveled around, shrugging, a small smile tugging at her lips. "It wasn't that. Those people aren't exactly my usual crowd. I'd expected to feel out of place. But I didn't."

Her posture had changed, subtly, only for an instant, but her uncertainty spoke volumes to him. And he felt ashamed. He'd been concerned about her seeming out of place, too. And how it would reflect on him.

Of course, he'd been equally concerned about Gina and her reaction.

Disgusted at his shallowness, he sighed. Sitting here now, after a successful evening, he could rationalize all he wanted. He was still a jerk.

Gina gave him a funny look, and he realized she was reacting to his sigh of disgust. Her smile widened. But it wasn't her usual bright, happy one. It was more sad and resigned. "It's okay, Jackson. I'm sure the thought crossed your mind, too. After all, last night was business."

He started to deny the innocuous charge, but he already felt lower than a belly-crawling snake. "Sometimes those affairs are tricky. All that protocol and crap," he said, telling himself the explanation was more for her benefit than his. But still he couldn't meet her eyes.

Glancing with purpose at his cluttered desk, his attention snagged on a pink message slip. He picked it up and held it out to her. "By the way, Diana Frost called. She wants you to contact her to meet for a drink or coffee. I told her you may be leaving for Switzerland today."

"*May* be leaving for Switzerland?" Gina shot him a dark look and grabbed the message slip. "I'd better be leaving today."

He was surprised at the disappointment her adamant desire to leave caused him. "It's in Greta's hands," he said, "so don't go flinging any darts this way."

At his abrupt tone, she looked up from the message. Her puzzled look was quickly replaced with one of contrition. "You don't usually even get involved in this sort of stuff, do you?"

"What stuff?" he asked slowly, realizing he may have just dug himself a hole.

"Someone losing their passport."

He shrugged and dragged out a stack of folders from his in-box, as if he didn't have enough paper making chaos out of his generally well-ordered desk. "Greta needed a hand."

Gina added to his sudden discomfort by tilting her head to the side and giving him a long, assessing look. Finally, she said, "You're a nice man, Jackson Maxwell Covington III."

Shaking his head, he laughed. He leaned back in his black leather chair and shoved a hand through his hair.

At the humorless sound, she straightened and her eyebrows drew together in admonition. "You are."

Never before in his life had he gotten involved in

such trivial embassy business. He hadn't done it because he was nice. Or because Greta was a personal friend. Or because he was some kind of knight in shining armor.

He'd gotten involved because he'd been attracted to Gina.

With the sudden secret admission, his insides coiled like a cornered snake about to strike, the denial and self-abhorrence so strong that it made him clench his jaw.

He cleared his throat, shuffled some paper. "You were sick. Greta was tied to her desk. I did what any other embassy staffer would or should do."

"Then you got me out of jail."

"Someone had to."

"And let me stay in your apartment."

She was starting to get on his nerves. He slammed a stack of folders back into the in-box. No way was he going to get to them today. Not with her yapping. "I couldn't throw you out in the street." He raised his gaze purposefully to hers. "But I'm thinking about it right now."

Her delighted laughter further annoyed him. No one had ever been immune to the warning look he'd just given her. "Why don't you just accept the compliment, Jack. You're a nice man."

Once again, he leaned back in his chair and raked a slow, cool gaze over her, letting it linger briefly on the curve of her breasts beneath the distracting salmon-colored T-shirt. When he got to her legs—bare, slightly tanned and inspiring a dampness at the back of his neck—he had to cut himself off. The game was over. He raised his gaze to meet hers.

She didn't say anything, and her expression revealed

not even a hint of her reaction to his foolish attempt to disconcert her.

She thought he was *nice*. He laughed to himself and seriously considered shocking her with the truth. That he'd thought about her far too much from the first moment he'd laid eyes on her. That if she were willing, he wouldn't think twice about clearing the desk with the back of his hand, laying her across it and ripping off her clothes with his teeth.

He wanted to see her breasts bare, wanted to feel her nipples blossom in his mouth. He wanted those long, tempting legs wrapped around his hips.

Most of all, he wanted her to get on that plane to Switzerland before he damn well blew a very promising career.

Chapter Ten

"I'm sorry. I did everything I could," Greta said, the regret in her voice suspiciously absent from her eyes. "But I do have your passport, at least. I just can't surrender it to you until the charges are formally dropped."

Gina squinted from Greta to Jack. He sat back in his chair looking at the other woman with a perplexed expression Gina couldn't interpret. "What if I demand my passport? Legally, it's mine, right?"

"Actually," Greta said, "it's considered property of the United States. And my being an official representative—"

"Well, if you ask me, this smacks of conspiracy."

Jack snorted, threw his hands up in the air. "Don't look at me. I'm as anxious for you to get on that plane as you are."

Greta looked at him with open disbelief.

Gina simply shrugged and tried to not let her hurt feelings show. Not that she was surprised that he wanted to get rid of her. He'd been acting funny for the past three hours. Apparently he didn't like being called nice. Well, the hell with him. She'd thought about telling him she'd reconsidered, that he wasn't very nice at all, but he'd probably like that.

Obviously he preferred being considered a tyrant, rudely barking orders at people, and suddenly displaying such appalling telephone manners that even poor Marcy looked reluctant to come in and give him his mail.

"You can't possibly be more anxious than I am, Bucko." Gina crossed her arms, catching Greta's amused expression before aiming a scowl at Jack.

"I'm certain that by tomorrow we can clear this up. In the meantime," Greta said, arching a disapproving brow at him, "may I suggest you not act like a horse's ass? You need another dinner partner for tonight."

Gina's brain registered the astonishment in Jack's face just about the same time shock zapped her. She giggled, something she often did when she got nervous. Both Jack and Greta turned to stare at her.

She pressed her lips together, then asked, "Did you just call him a horse's ass?"

A flush spread across Greta's cheeks, and she patted the tight bun she wore at her nape. Hesitantly her gaze returned to Jack. "I don't know what's gotten into you," she said, a slightly defensive edge to her tone.

"Me?" He frowned and gave a small shake of his head. "You really aren't going to that dinner with me tonight," he said, and she confirmed his bleak statement with a shake of her own. "Even though you know how important tonight is to me."

"I'm not doing this to punish you," she said evenly. "Something unexpected came up. I'm terribly sorry."

He rubbed the side of his jaw, his gaze straying distractedly out the window. "Forget it. I've been, uh..." He let his voice trail off, continuing to stare outside for a couple of seconds before turning a weary face in Greta's direction. "You've been a real trouper about accompanying me to these events, and I've taken you for granted. I'm sorry. Nevertheless, I've really appreciated your company.''

Greta blinked, her expression briefly softening. She refocused her pale green eyes on Jack and sent him a faint smile. ''I have never felt taken for granted by you, Jackson. Not for a minute.''

Gina quickly pushed off the sofa and rose to her feet. It was time for her to take another walk, even though she'd already taken four today and it was way too hot to be pounding the pavement.

She felt like a voyeur, watching these two people declare their silent admiration for each other. Although it didn't surprise her. After all, she knew about Greta's having the hots for him since the first day she'd arrived. Gina simply hadn't expected to be standing here when they finally admitted their feelings. Nor had she expected the irrational stab of jealousy that made getting to her feet so difficult.

''Well, I'll see you two later—''

Both of them turned toward her at the same time. ''Sit down,'' they said in unison.

Stunned at their abruptness, she sat.

''Gina can go with you again tonight,'' Greta said, already having turned back to Jack after glancing at her watch. ''She can borrow the dress I was going to wear. We can go to my apartment right now before siesta is over.''

Talk about feeling taken for granted, Gina thought as she stared with growing irritation at the woman. She was about to make a crack when Jack beat her to it.

''I think we need to ask Gina first,'' he said, with a wry twist to his mouth. Transferring his gaze to her, he waited for her to answer.

She folded her arms across her chest. She should tell them both to shove it. And then she remembered that Greta was in love with Jack, and that some kind of emergency had obviously come up, forcing her to make this sacrifice.

Well, Gina was no martyr. Going with Jack tonight would be a sacrifice for her, too. She had nothing in common with these people. She had to watch every word that came out of her mouth. She'd have to wear another beautiful dress, undoubtedly eat a sinfully rich dessert worthy of being placed in some art museum.

And dance with the man who could make her body and resolve melt faster than a scoop of vanilla ice cream under a stream of piping hot fudge.

Oh, hell.

She met two pairs of impatient eyes. "I'm thinking," she barked.

Jack let out a loud resigned sigh. "Never mind. I can't ask you to do this again."

"Yes, you can," Greta said, turning to Gina. "What else would you have to do tonight?"

She gave a casual shrug. "Oh, I don't know. I was thinking maybe I'd cruise Via Veneto and, you know, turn a few tricks."

Jack gave her a double-take.

Greta burst out laughing. "Come on, Gina. Let's leave now while there's no traffic." She walked to the door, clearly for her, the problem solved.

"I don't know if this is a good idea," Jack said, getting to his feet.

Greta had already opened the door. She looked him squarely in the eyes. "Why?"

Gina had stood again, and when he looked to her for support, she said nothing. She was interested in his an-

swer, too. He'd said tonight was important to him.
Maybe too important for someone like her to accompany him.

"Because Gina obviously doesn't want to go and
you're strong-arming her."

He was lying. Gina could tell by the way he'd visibly
swallowed right before he answered. And the nervous
way he played with the end of his tie was another small
giveway. But mostly, she could tell by the way he refused to look at her.

"That's not true," she said. "I'd love to go."

The satisfaction she received from the grim misgiving
in his expression was small. She'd also just lied. Any
former thrill she'd felt at being his date again had disappeared.

"YOU'RE SURE ABOUT THIS dress?" Gina asked Greta
when they were less than five minutes away from Jack's
apartment.

The other woman didn't laugh as she had the first
and second time Gina had asked the same question. Instead, she gave Gina a disgusted look before resuming
concentration on the road ahead.

"I didn't see anyone wearing this color last night,"
Gina persisted, recalling that she had actually seen one
red dress. On Brigitte. Which was what worried Gina.
But at the risk of sounding like a snob, she didn't share
that concern with Greta. "Most of the women wore
black or cream. Nothing this bright."

Greta shot her an annoyed look, designed, no doubt,
to shut Gina up once and for all. "Are you questioning
my taste?"

"Well..." Gina shifted uncomfortably in her seat.

Greta drove an incredibly small car for being so tall. "Yeah."

"Yes, you are questioning my taste?" Greta glanced at her in surprise, then chuckled. "I have attended dozens of these dinners with Jackson. I assure you I am not steering you wrong. After all, I was going to wear that dress myself."

Gina eyed the provocative little number lying in plastic across her lap. Vivid red silk, with a plunging neckline and scooped-out back, it didn't look like anything Greta would even glance at on a store rack, much less try on. Apparently there was a side to Greta that Gina didn't know about. Which was a stupid thought. She didn't know this woman at all.

She only knew that Greta wanted Jack.

She slid the woman another look and said, "I didn't mean to insult you. I just don't want to embarrass Jack."

Greta continued to look straight ahead. If she was surprised by Gina's honesty, she showed no reaction, except for a small twitch at the corner of her mouth. Or maybe she realized Gina wasn't being quite so noble and understood what she was really doing—trying to jolt some information out of Greta.

"You won't embarrass Jackson," she finally said with amazing confidence. "I can promise you that."

"Don't be so sure," Gina mumbled. "You're used to these kinds of dinners."

Greta pulled the car into an illegal spot in front of Jackson's apartment and turned wide eyes on Gina. "You really are worried."

"I wouldn't call it worried—" she began, hating the old feelings of inferiority that were seeping in without warning.

Greta had angled around to look at her, shaking her head in open wonder. "Look at you, Gina. You're beautiful, poised, quick-witted...." She kept shaking her head, ignoring Gina's struggle to not choke to death.

Quick-witted Gina could live with. She had to be fast on the uptake. She had four obnoxious brothers and she was from Brooklyn. But poised? Beautiful?

"Don't sell yourself short, Gina. That's the biggest disservice you could ever do."

Gina had to bite her lip. Any remark she made was bound to sound unkind. By failing to make her feelings clear to Jack, Greta was guilty of not practicing what she preached.

"You're going to look beautiful in that dress, and unless I miss my guess, Jackson won't be feeling anything except frustrated for not being able to string two coherent thoughts together."

The gleeful glint in the older woman's eyes brought Gina's distracted thoughts up short, and she narrowed her gaze at Greta. "I don't think I follow you."

Alarm flickered, then died so quickly in Greta's face that Gina almost thought she'd imagined it. Almost.

She rested a hand on Greta's arm. "If you're trying to make him jealous, I've gotta tell you, you're going about this all wrong."

Greta laughed until her eyes misted. "I have no designs on Jackson Covington." She dabbed at her lashes. "Is that what you think?" She laughed again. "Jackson and I have known each other since boarding school. He's turned into a fine man and I care a lot about him." She shook her head. "Just not that way."

Gina was stunned. She'd been so certain, had even felt guilty for having lustful thoughts about him herself.

Now what? What was she supposed to feel and think now?

And what the hell did Greta think she was doing?

Gina was about to ask just that when a cop pulled up in front of their illegally parked car.

Spotting him, Greta slipped the car into gear. "Time to scoot, dear. I can't afford another ticket."

Gina hopped out and watched Greta speed away, her head spinning, her thoughts rudderless, until an odd crinkling sound captured her attention. Seeking the source, she stared down at her shaky hands, clenching the plastic-covered dress.

Tonight was starting to feel like a real date.

BRINGING HER WITH HIM tonight had been a mistake. If Jackson had been thinking clearly, he would have realized what a folly it was to be spending any more time with her as soon as Greta had suggested it. But he'd let his overactive imagination get in the way of good sense. The desk fantasy had been the first one to set him off. From there it hadn't been difficult to imagine her stretched out on his office sofa, his kitchen table, the rug in front of the living room fireplace. His bed.

And now he was being punished for his foolishness by having to sit here and watch her in that red dress. Even worse, he had to sit here and watch James Worthington watch her in that dress while she laughed and joked with Jonathan and Diana Frost.

Jackson downed his Scotch and passed his empty glass back to the bartender for another. By now, the man knew how he liked it. Straight, neat and fast. But this was it, Jackson told himself. Two drinks were normally his limit. Tonight he'd pushed that limit to three, but he had to stop. One more and he'd be tempted to punch James Worthington in his royal nose.

And Jackson hardly thought the consul general would be tolerant of one of his assistants flattening a British duke. Even if the man was an amoral, double-talking, ladies' man who neglected his own date while he flirted shamelessly with Gina.

Not that she had invited his attention. If anything, she'd tried to ignore him. But that dress was like a damn magnet....

Hell, it wasn't just the dress. It was Gina. There was something different about her tonight. Her smile was even more radiant than usual, and her eyes so vividly alive that whenever they touched him, heat stirred in his belly like a volcano about to erupt.

She seemed more confident, more carefree, almost invincible, as though she had nothing to lose. Which was true. Tonight was merely a way for her to pass time. Tomorrow she'd be gone. From Rome. From his life.

The thought produced an unexpected and disturbing knot in his stomach, and he wasn't sure what proved the greater source of his irritation—that she would be leaving, or that she seemed anxious to do so.

He shouldn't care. Her attendance here with him should mean nothing more than if it were Greta offering to pitch in. But he'd be a liar not to admit otherwise. Something had changed since their dance last night, since he'd held her in his arms, since he'd pulled out every stop to keep from kissing her when he'd deposited her at her bedroom door.

But that was last night. Before tonight was over, he *would* kiss her. And as bad an idea as that was, he'd be damned if he knew what to do about it.

He brought his drink to his lips, threw back his head, then slid the empty glass across the bar. When the bartender lifted the bottle of twelve-year-old Scotch for a refill, Jackson held up a restraining hand and shook his head. He chuckled wryly to himself. How ironic that he'd fleetingly worried last night about Gina being out of place, that she might blow things for him, he thought as he slid Worthington a glance. One more drink and Jackson would be the one to blow it himself tonight.

After adjusting his bow tie, he headed toward Gina and the Frosts. With great satisfaction, he positioned himself behind Gina, effectively blocking Worthington's view of her naked back.

She turned to frown at him. "What are you doing back there?"

He lifted a shoulder. "I didn't want to interrupt your conversation."

Smiling, she twisted around and slipped an arm around his waist to guide him into the circle. "You big dope," she whispered so that only he could hear. "You aren't interrupting anything. I was just telling some of my more colorful courier stories."

He smiled back, acknowledging that tonight he really was a dope, but he liked the feel of her body so close to his, and when she started to pull away, he trapped her arm so that she had little choice but to maintain contact or cause a scene.

Her startled gaze briefly probed his before Diana Frost reclaimed her attention. Once she became engaged in conversation, Gina relaxed against him and he stood quietly, inhaling the fresh almond scent of her hair.

What exactly had changed since last night? For that matter, why did this party seem different from the others? Many of the same dinner guests were in attendance tonight, the same crowd he often saw weekly. Although each host tended to try to outdo the others, the same premium liquor stocked the bars, the same species of white-gloved waiters passed artful and exotic tidbits, and the background orchestra music was always flawless. But something was unquestionably different.

For one thing, there was laughter. More laughter than this somewhat stuffy crowd generally engaged in. And it all centered around Gina.

His lips curved with an absurd burst of proprietary pride. Then he blinked, his smile slowly fading as he realized this wasn't just about Gina. He felt different, too.

He felt alive.

The absence of a glass in his hand made him cast a longing look at the Scotch bottle behind the bar. He wouldn't indulge his sudden edginess, though. He had too much at stake. Bad enough that he cared astonishingly little about his career at the moment. He should be mingling. He should be keeping an eye out for the ambassador.

All he wanted to do was watch Gina.

She was charming everyone, just like he'd known she would. He had a feeling Gina rarely met a stranger.

He envied that quality. He wasn't gregarious by nature, which spoke poorly for someone in his profession. Being sociable, diplomatic and political were all tools of his trade, tools he'd struggled to acquire and maintain. And for the most part, he'd overcome the handicap of wanting to chuck the small talk and go sit in a corner. But he still hated coming to these dinners alone, and he was grateful he had Gina here with him. Not just because she was a warm body. But because she was Gina.

The fine tinkle of a sterling silver bell at the hands

of a white-gloved, white-jacketed waiter wove through the crowd and everyone immediately moved toward the dining room. For most of the guests this dinner was no more significant than the many others they all attended with sometimes annoying frequency, but for Jackson, tonight was especially important.

The United States ambassador was making one of his infrequent appearances, along with two important senators who held a lot of weight regarding embassy matters. This was the political aspect of the job Jackson despised, but if he wanted to stay in the game, he had to remain a player.

Briefly he'd thought about warning Gina, but ended up deciding that the knowledge would probably make her nervous. On the other hand, he doubted she gave a flip, rightfully so, about his career, which meant the information would mean nothing to her, anyway.

And then he realized that he needn't worry. Gina was doing just fine. Red dress and all.

He still didn't understand the dress. It definitely wasn't Greta's style, yet he knew she'd lent it to Gina. In his opinion, it even bordered on inappropriate for tonight. But he trusted Greta's taste, and with the exception of that idiot Worthington and two other slobbering Spanish delegates, the dress didn't seem to be a problem.

Gina spotted their place cards first, and he was relieved to see her name scripted in gold and not Miranda's. He'd had Marcy call ahead to make sure the name had been changed on the guest list. He didn't want to think about Miranda tonight, much less have Gina question him about her. If she did, he wasn't sure what he would say.

As soon as he pulled out her chair, he saw James

Worthington stop at the table setting opposite Gina. Staring down at the place card, the man smiled and raised his gaze to Gina, its intensity bordering on insolence.

"How fortuitous for me," he said, bowing slightly but deliberately holding her gaze. "I'm allowed to sit across from the most beautiful woman here."

His pretty blond companion blinked and glanced away. All the men at the table had remained standing until the women were seated, and the fellow to her right quickly pulled out her chair. She sent him a grateful smile.

Worthington ignored them both. He pulled out his own chair, sent a fleeting glance down the long crystal-laden table and, seeing that all the women were now seated, lowered himself to his place, his practiced smile centered on Gina.

With growing irritation, Jackson watched her lips curve in response. Except it wasn't her usual smile. It was polite but forced, and he suddenly thought he would give just about anything to hear what she truly wanted to say to the royal pain in the ass.

His annoyance dissolved, and he had to hide a grin just thinking of the possibilities. Under the table, he touched her arm. At first she seemed reluctant to break eye contact with Worthington, which gave Jackson pause, but then he realized it was one of her "Bucko" looks she was giving the duke, and Jackson had to tamp down a chuckle.

Finally, she blinked and turned toward Jackson.

He lowered his mouth near her ear and asked, "Want me to punch him in the nose?"

He hadn't meant to say that, but when she laughed

out loud and her eyes lit with their familiar sparkle, he was glad he had.

"And deprive me of the pleasure?" She flashed him a mischievous look that raised more than one red flag. "I don't think so."

His sudden misgiving must have shown, because she laughed again, patted his thigh and said, "Don't worry. I'm going to behave myself." She slid an innocent glance at Worthington before leveling her gaze with Jackson's. "Even if it kills me."

Merriment danced in her brown eyes, and the corners of her mouth curved in devilish amusement. She didn't look away. She stayed focused on him as if wanting to prolong their private joke.

And Jackson couldn't help staring back, captivated by her uninhibited humor, her barely concealed restraint. The imprint of her hand on his thigh had remained long after she'd withdrawn her heat, and he, unwisely, without a shred of regard for his duty as an embassy representative, was tempted to say "screw dinner."

"So, Jackson..." The intrusion of James Worthington's suave, cultured British voice was as welcome as a bucket of ice cold water. "Tell me something," he said slowly, waiting for Jackson to break eye contact with Gina.

Even at the risk of appearing rude, Jackson was in no rush. His eyes held Gina's a moment longer, hoping they told her more than he could articulate right now. Tonight would not end like last night. No rushed, awkward good nights in the foyer with averted glances and rigid postures. Tonight would be special. Tonight they would...

"Covington?" The annoyance in Worthington's

voice was plain, and several other couples engaged in private conversations turned their way.

Reluctantly, Jackson met Worthington's gaze with a blank expression.

Worthington settled back in his chair, clearly pleased with his new audience. "I was simply wondering," he said, with an innocent lift of his dark eyebrows, "where you were keeping Miranda these days."

From his peripheral vision, Jackson saw another couple exchange glances. It was clear Worthington was not the only one wondering about Miranda.

"You know better than that, Worthington," Jackson said as flatly as he could. "No one keeps Miranda anywhere." He leaned back to allow a waiter access to his wineglass and saw that there was no one at the table more interested than Gina. Ignoring her anxious gaze, he shrugged casually and added, "I believe she's in Ireland, or maybe Belgium. I'm not sure."

Worthington laughed. "Oh, come now. You know precisely where she is. Miranda would see to that."

Several of the other men who also knew Miranda laughed, too, until their wives gave them disapproving looks.

"You're probably right," Jackson said, wondering how he was going to gracefully get out of this conversation. "Which means my secretary very likely knows where she is. I'll be happy to have her give you a call if you're trying to get in touch with Miranda."

The impersonal way in which he spoke about his frequent companion raised more than one pair of eyebrows and inflicted upon him no small amount of guilt, but he figured the evasion would be worth it if he escaped an inquisition from Gina.

Worthington's date whispered something to him, derailing his attention from the conversation. And when Jackson noticed that Gina was busy smiling at the waiter who poured her wine, he started to breathe a sigh of relief.

As soon as the man turned to fill the next glass, Jackson felt her hand on his thigh. She lightly stroked the ridge of muscle stretching toward his groin and his relief turned into arousal.

Leaning toward him, her breath tickling his cheek, she asked, "Who's Miranda?"

Chapter Eleven

Gina frowned when Jack pretended he hadn't heard her. She pinched the area just above his knee, and when he turned to glare at her, she smiled sweetly. "Who is Miranda?" she repeated.

"A friend of mine."

"I figured that much out for myself."

He sipped his wine.

"Well?"

He blinked at her. "Well what?"

She couldn't tell if he was deliberately being obtuse or not. She was used to men who routinely gave one-syllable answers when they could get away with it. "Tell me more."

"What's to tell?"

"I don't know," she said through gritted teeth, her patience slipping away quicker than air from a popped balloon. "That's why I asked the question."

He sighed, the sound filled with disgust.

Tough. His evasiveness was making her twice as curious. She elbowed him.

He stared at her with his seductive blue eyes, and her stubborn resolve stuttered.

"Sometimes she comes to these dinners with me," he finally said.

"Does she work for the embassy?"

"No."

Gina took a deep breath, silently debating with herself whether she should push for more information. There was no sense spoiling her last evening here just to satisfy her own nosiness. Except she knew a need more than curiosity was fueling her determination. Jack was hiding something, and Gina sensed it involved her. And if that something had to do with another woman, a woman he was committed to...

She ordered herself to calm down. So what if he had a girlfriend? Jack had asked her to accompany him as a favor. No romantic promises or advances had been made.

So then why did he look guilty as sin?

The same look Nick had had only three days ago.

The memory of Nick made the hair on the back of Gina's neck reach for the ceiling, and she had to tell herself to calm down all over again. Jack had made no promises, she reminded herself. But of course, neither had Nick. And the truth of that depressed her. She didn't want to think she was that stupid about men. Maybe when she was younger and more gullible, but not now.

She wasn't going to ask Jack another question about the mysterious Miranda. The woman was none of her business. And neither was Jackson Maxwell Covington III.

GINA WAS AMAZED at how much she was beginning to like dancing. Of course, having Jack's arms around her had a lot to do with her new passion. On two different occasions she'd been cornered into dancing with other men, and the awkwardness of her lack of skills aside, the experience hadn't been nearly as pleasant as when Jack pressed his palm to her lower back, or when she felt his heartbeat, strong and steady, against her right breast.

In the middle of a bluesy number, she tilted her head back and looked up at him and, as expected, was promptly rewarded with the caress of his sensual blue gaze and slow, heart-stopping smile. His hand tightened at the small of her back, and she reflexively pressed her breasts into his chest. It was a tiny movement, nearly imperceptible, but his eyes darkened with a desire so thick it made her knees weak, and she moved her head so that her cheek rested against his shoulder and she no longer had to look into those tempting eyes that made her forget how this night was supposed to end. Chaste. Businesslike. Without regret.

They were probably too close for propriety's sake, in her opinion, but Jack didn't seem to care. So obviously the intimacy she felt was only in her own mind. Because if anything, Jack was politically and socially correct. She'd watched him a lot tonight, talking to the French ambassador, laughing at the dignitary's wife's anecdotes, shaking hands with other diplomats and working the room like a pro.

The experience made her both proud and sad, even though she had no right to either feeling. Tomorrow she'd be in Switzerland, and after that she'd be flying back to Brooklyn. And either Greta or the illusive Miranda would be sitting beside Jack at the next dinner.

The thought depressed her more than she cared to admit and she pressed closer still, seeking his warmth and reassurance that at least for tonight, she still had him to...

Gina blinked.

Something wasn't right in the way they...fit.

Suspiciously, she shifted, while trying to keep in step with him, but she faltered and he prevented her from stumbling by hauling her against his body a little more roughly than he'd probably intended.

And she knew instantly what the problem was. Jack was harder than a Trevi Fountain statue.

Her heart slammed against her chest, and her pulse exploded into a rhythm so fierce it stung her veins and sent a prickly tingling sensation down her spine. Her immediate impulse was to look into his face, but she fought the urge and averted her eyes. Her willpower lasted two seconds before she slowly pulled back and met his unrepentant gaze.

His lips curved in a slow, knowing smile, and she missed another step. He used the situation to gather her closer still. And God help her, she wanted to feel his arousal again, wanted to bask in knowing what she did to him.

Her thighs squeezed against his until she felt him, solid and inciting, a shaft of heat and hardness burning through her dress, scorching her lower belly. In her ears, the music was no longer a waltz but a primal jungle beat.

There was no way he didn't know how much he'd excited her. Her heart was pounding so wildly she was surprised something didn't pop out of her dress. She had to monitor her breathing, remember to breathe at all. And she had to stop looking into his eyes. The raw desire she found simmering there fascinated her, compelled her...frightened the hell out of her.

If she were as smart as she thought she was, she'd leave. Right now. Before the hand struck midnight. But his palm, still flush against her naked back, was creating a pleasant friction with her skin, and the tips of his fingers nestled between her vertebrae kept her a willing captive more effectively than any barred cell could.

The sensation of being touched was all-encompassing, as if there was no place sacred, no place he wasn't in contact with, no place he couldn't reach if he chose. Where there was no actual physical connection, moist heat erupted and excited her.

She'd caught him looking at her a lot tonight, whether he was across the room or beside her at the dinner table. Several times the intensity of his gaze had disconcerted her, and she realized now the entire evening had been a kind of foreplay.

And if she weren't careful, the climax wasn't too far into the future.

Shifting back, she ran the tip of her tongue across her suddenly parched lips and glanced around the room. Incredibly, no one paid them any attention, despite the fact that they no longer kept in time to the music. Their bodies barely swayed, their movements so slow she was shocked not to find every pair of eyes upon them.

But the dance floor was crowded with couples engaged in private conversations, and she couldn't help but wonder what might have happened had they been dancing in his living room instead of a public place.

At the tantalizing thought, a telling shiver rippled across her shoulders, and her gaze automatically flew to his fathomless eyes. She found no smugness there, no apology or hesitance. Only longing.

She looked away, stiffening her boneless body, and her gaze collided with Brigitte's.

The fact that someone was actually watching them, after all, startled some sense into her and she straightened further, putting another few inches between them. But the woman's shy glance quickly slipped away just as it had before dinner when Gina had first spotted her.

"Is anything wrong?" Jack asked in such a cool, composed voice that it sparked a surge of indignation in Gina before it injected her, too, with a boost of confidence.

Especially since she knew that underneath all that self-assurance he was still harder than a rock.

She lifted her shoulder in a small shrug. "What could be wrong?"

He eyed her skeptically. "Maybe you'd like to stop and have something cool to drink?"

He was acting so damned normal it gave her pause, and she backed up another step when the orchestra tarried between songs. She couldn't possibly have just imagined his reaction. Could she?

She narrowed her gaze at him. "I think you're the one who needs something cold."

Jack laughed so loud, several people turned and stared. "Actually, I had something else in mind. Come on."

He grabbed her hand and started to leave the dance floor, and she froze, half afraid he'd haul her back to the privacy of his apartment, half afraid he wouldn't.

"Gina?" He turned amused eyes at her. "Are you asking me for the next dance?"

She made a face, instead of the wisecrack that tempted her, then let him lead her off the floor. "Where are we going?" she asked, her voice slightly breathless when she saw they were headed for a secluded corner of the room.

"There's someone I want you to meet."

Disappointment slithered through her, and then curiosity took over and she glanced around. The only person she recognized in the small cluster of people ahead of them was the United States ambassador. Surely Jack didn't want her to meet someone like him—in effect, Jack's boss.

She tugged at the bodice of her dress, wishing the neckline was an inch higher, that the slit along her thigh had ended somewhere closer to her knee. And she told herself she would not greet the ambassador by bursting out with the information that this was really Greta's dress.

She stopped suddenly, and Jack did, too, his startled gaze meeting hers.

"What's the matter?" he asked slowly.

"Who do you want me to meet?"

At the defensiveness in her voice, his face creased in a frown. "The ambassador."

"Why?"

He blinked, looking puzzled. "He's an interesting man, great sense of humor, very well traveled, just as you are." He shrugged, clearly at a loss. "I don't know. It just occurred to me you might have a lot in common."

She laughed. "Right."

He blinked again, his gaze flicking away, and she knew she'd planted a seed of doubt. His hesitancy shouldn't have wounded her since she was the one who'd pointed out the folly of his assumption. And she was flattered that he'd even considered introducing her. But maybe she wasn't ready for this.

"I'd really rather make a trip to the powder room if it's all the same to you," she said with a breezy wave of her hand. "He looks like he's in the middle of something, anyway."

"Of course," he said with a slight bow of his head that made him seem so much more like Jackson than Jack. "In the meantime, what can I get you?"

She teased him with a slow, provocative smile that ended up ruffling her more than it did him when his eyes met hers and darkened. He didn't smile, in fact he wore no expression. But of course he didn't have to reveal his thoughts. His eyes plainly told her their little sensual tango on the dance floor hadn't ended. Not by a long shot.

"Surprise me," she muttered, and headed in the opposite direction.

She didn't really have to powder her nose or do anything else other than grab a brief time-out away from Jack. She smiled at several couples she passed along the way, surprised when they knew her name. Hobnobbing with these people for the past two nights had turned out to be amazingly easy. It helped that Jack was such a considerate companion, quick to introduce her or include her in conversations. She'd never once felt out of place, even when the dialogue had turned political or the topic had soared over her head.

Jack always made sure she was comfortable. There had even been times during the evening when she'd imagined that he'd gazed at her with pride when she'd contributed her opinion. Which of course was ridiculous because he had no reason to feel that way, and certainly nothing at stake. Not really.

She smiled to herself. He'd even wanted to introduce her to the ambassador. She was the one who'd wimped out.

And who wouldn't, in this red dress?

Stifling a groan, she inconspicuously hiked up her bodice again. It was still hard to believe this was something Greta would wear. Although this was a dress Gina herself may have picked out only a week ago, after seeing the truly elegant array of understated dresses last night, she had to admit she'd have made a different choice today.

Her tastes hadn't changed exactly, and she certainly wasn't trying to suit Jack, she assured herself as she left the ballroom, although she didn't have a ready answer for her change of heart, either.

The foyer was mainly empty, with the exception of a waiter and a trio of cigar-smoking gray-haired men standing near the hall leading to the powder room. Nestled in the curve of the three-story staircase was a sitting area. Four green brocade upholstered chairs sat on an Oriental rug and were grouped around a mahogany table polished to such a high shine that bright light reflected off it from the staircase chandelier.

And sitting in the far corner by herself was Brigitte. Her eyes were downcast as she stirred the contents of a gold-rimmed china cup, and Gina's first thought was to hurry past before Brigitte saw her. But her conscience got in the way and slowed her down long enough for the blonde to glance up. Her lips immediately curved in a hopeful smile, and Gina's heart thudded.

She sighed. Jack was waiting for her. She really didn't want to get involved in a conversation right now. *Especially not with her.*

The small, snooty voice blindsided Gina, and she winced with self-disgust. Even though she really didn't want to get stuck talking to Brigitte. It wasn't that there was anything *wrong* with the woman. Of course, Gina would not have chosen a gold lamé dress, or rhinestone shoes, or...

Oh, God, who was she kidding? She was being a damned snob, and maybe worse, a fraud. Sitting with Brigitte wasn't going to make her look bad. After all, how much worse could talking with someone make a sanctimonious hypocrite look?

Gina came to a stop and smiled back. But to her further disgust, she automatically glanced over her bare shoulder before approaching the other woman.

"Gina, right?" Brigitte's eyes lit up at Gina's advance, obviously pleased with the promise of company, and managed to make Gina feel lower than an ant.

"Right," Gina said. "And you're Brigitte?"

The blonde nodded. "Please, sit."

Gina hadn't heard her say much last night and noticed that although she spoke readily in English, her French accent was very pronounced. Up close, she was also much younger than Gina had originally thought, the heavy-handed makeup adding years to her face. Sitting here, idly stirring her drink, she looked as though she were barely out of her teens, lonely and not a little forlorn.

Once again, shame doused Gina with remorse, and she lowered herself to one of the chairs. "Why aren't you dancing?"

Brigitte's face fell and she gave a small shrug. "My fiancé has business to discuss."

Gina smiled. "This is supposed to be a social occasion."

The blonde scrunched her perfect little nose. Then comprehension dawned, and she widened her black-rimmed, sad blue eyes and sighed. "Yes, but it is always business first with him. I understand."

No, she didn't. She wanted his attention. She wanted to feel like she belonged to this group who greeted one another with air kisses at both cheeks and politely inquired about one another's children before they went on to solve the problems of the world.

Gina had seen the woman's yearning looks last night, the quick but uncertain smiles she flashed when jokes had been told at dinner. Gina understood well, because six years ago, she had been in Brigitte's place. Wanting to get as far away from her Brooklyn roots as possible, she'd pranced out on that lonely and unknown limb, deathly afraid she'd fall on her face, but more afraid she'd be stuck in some two-bedroom brownstone for the rest of her life, eating off chipped white ceramic plates, redeemed from green stamps for faithfully buying her weekly groceries from the same market.

Even tonight, she didn't belong in this environment any more than Brigitte did, but now she was more jaded and militant about the entire damn class system. She'd found another way out of the monotony her siblings so easily accepted. And except for the occasional twinges of feeling "less than," she had reconciled those awkward emotional upheavals. But she hadn't forgotten how vastly intimidating it felt to be the outcast.

Gina met Brigitte's grateful eyes and felt bad all over again for trying to ignore the woman.

"I like your dress," Brigitte said with a shy tilt of her head. "And last night's dress, too."

Gina smiled. What was one little white lie? "Your dress, too," she said. "It's very—"

Brigitte briskly shook her head and plucked at the gold lamé. "Giorgio was very unhappy with this," she whispered. "He did not like last night's dress, and he does not like that I have nothing important to say. He almost left me at home.''

At the woman's obvious distress, Gina blinked. Okay, so she wasn't crazy about the dress, either, but screw Giorgio. She covered Brigitte's hand. "If I were hanging around for any more of these dinners, I think I'd stick to basic black myself. And maybe a little more material,'' she added, with an upward tug at her too-low neckline.

Brigitte wrinkled her nose again, and Gina wasn't sure if she simply didn't understand, or was upset by Gina's subtle but unsolicited advice. But then a smile returned to her lips, and Gina realized it was probably only a communication problem.

She sat back, withdrawing her hand, and Brigitte's eyes widened with a hint of panic.

Gina opened her mouth to assure her she wasn't leaving just yet, but before she could get a word out, Brigitte said quickly, "I know how to hang a spoon from my nose.''

Gina laughed, certain she'd not heard correctly.

Brigitte flushed.

Gina shrugged and made an international expression of helplessness. "Pardon me?''

"I can hang a spoon from my nose. It is easy,'' Brigitte said, smiling again when she assumed Gina simply hadn't heard.

Gina glanced suspiciously at the contents the blonde was stirring in the cup. She got a brief whiff of some kind of liqueur, but she was beginning to wonder if Brigitte was even old enough to drink. "Really?''

Her nod was enthusiastic as she pulled the spoon from her cup and began licking it dry. "I can show you.''

Gina choked back a cough. "That's okay. I believe you. Really." She slid a look over her shoulder and was relieved to find they were alone in the foyer.

Brigitte dug into her small gold purse and withdrew a white tissue. "You do this first," she said, and began scrubbing her nose. "To clear the makeup."

Penance. That's what this was, for being a snob earlier. Gina swallowed hard. She didn't want to offend Brigitte, but she sure as hell didn't want to sit here and talk to her with a spoon hanging off her nose.

She reached out to still the woman's hands, but Brigitte had already started to set her trick in motion, and to interfere could end up being even more disastrous.

Instead, Gina sat back, paranoia forcing her to glance over her shoulder. Thankfully, no one was in sight. Breathing a sigh of relief, she turned back to find Brigitte grinning behind a silver spoon, which, as predicted, hung precariously from the blonde's pert nose.

Gina failed to stifle her startled laugh.

Brigitte's grin widened as the spoon dropped into her lap. "See? It is easy."

"I see." Gina rubbed her palms together to keep herself from dragging them down the delicate silk of Greta's dress, glad the ordeal was over without incident.

"Do you want to try it?"

She froze at Brigitte's shy question and stared into her earnest blue eyes. "Uh, I don't think so."

Gina had tried to play it cool and didn't know what gave her growing alarm away, but the blonde stiffened, panic filling her eyes with the certain knowledge that she'd just committed a huge faux pas.

"I've got these freckles, you see," Gina said quickly. "They're all over my nose, and if I wipe off my makeup

I'll look like a real idiot, and I don't have any powder or foundation or anything—''

She broke off, holding her minuscule evening bag in midair as if to back up her claim. But it was obvious by the perplexed frown on Brigitte's face that Gina had rattled off too quickly and Brigitte didn't have a clue as to what she was talking about.

The blonde smiled. "It is easy," she said, passing Gina a tissue, then once again balancing the spoon off the end of her nose. Slowly, as if walking a circus tightrope, she held out both her hands. The spoon barely moved.

Out of the corner of her eye, Gina glimpsed Brigitte's fiancé, Giorgio. She turned her head slightly to get a better view of him and saw him scowling at Brigitte. He looked furious.

Obviously she didn't see him. Her gaze fastened on Gina, Brigitte's spurt of bubbly laughter caused the spoon to drop and she swept it up as it fell and offered it to Gina. "You try it."

At the look of horror on Giorgio's face, Gina cringed. Embarrassment, disappointment, anger all flashed like lightning across a midnight sky, and Gina knew Brigitte was in for a major chewing out. Old feelings surfaced suddenly, and she knew she couldn't let Brigitte face the humiliation alone.

Quickly, she rubbed a tissue across her nose, glanced past Giorgio to make sure the coast was clear and stuck the round part of the spoon onto her nose.

After only a few seconds, her first try succeeded.

When she glanced back at Giorgio, over his shoulder a pair of shocked blue eyes met hers.

Beside Jack, the United States ambassador bellowed with laughter.

Chapter Twelve

It was a long, silent ride home. Gina thought more than once about explaining what had happened to Jack. About how she'd felt badly for Brigitte because she understood the humiliation and self-reproach that would follow the not-so-smart spoon incident, and that she'd only wanted to soften the blow. And if she were totally honest, she'd admit that her reaction had been pure reflex, and if she'd had one rational thought in her head she would have simply grabbed the spoon away from Brigitte.

But Jack was in no mood for explanations. That was clear by the firm set of his jaw, the tight line of his lips, the way his eyebrows slanted angrily together.

Gina stared straight ahead and quit sending secret glances at his profile. For the most part, Gina wasn't even all that sure she wanted to offer any justification. It wasn't as if she'd committed a crime, for heaven's sake.

No. She didn't feel like giving him an explanation, after all.

Liar.

She sagged against the cool leather car seat, let her head fall to the side and watched the passing headlights zoom by. His anger she could deal with. It was the oppressive silence filled with disappointment and censure that made her want to crawl into bed, curl up into a ball and pull the covers over her head.

"Are you asleep?" he finally asked.

For a moment she thought about not answering him, letting him think she *was* asleep, but they'd be arriving at his apartment at any minute and she'd have to face him, anyway.

She rolled her head until she faced him. "Just thinking."

Lights from oncoming cars flashed across his face, and for the briefest moment, she saw the corner of his mouth hike up.

She sniffed. "Yeah, believe it or not, I do that sometimes."

"Think?" he asked with an innocence that curved her lips into a wry smile.

Gina looked away to study her polished fingertips. If he'd made a disparaging face, she didn't want to see it. "Look, do you want to hear an explanation, or not?"

"If you feel one is necessary."

"Stop it, Jackson."

He kept his eyes on the road, which she wasn't sure was for practical reasons or to irritate her. He was acting so much like...like...Jackson. She missed Jack.

"Haven't you ever been impulsive?" she asked, frustration with his high-handed manner creeping into her voice. "Or done something you later regretted, but which seemed right at the time? Or are you just that perfect?"

"I guess I'm just that perfect," he said as he turned the car into the underground garage.

She stared, openmouthed, appalled at his arrogance.

A second later, she let out a low, exasperated shriek that made him wince. It felt damn good. "You don't deserve an explanation."

He pulled the car to a stop, flipped off the engine and turned to her with a thunderous expression. She lifted her chin in challenge, but braced herself for his wrath, trying to decide how much of it she actually deserved. Not much, she decided, and lifted her chin higher.

A beam from the overhead garage light fell on Jack's chest and threw muted shadows across most of his face, but she could still see the angry slash of his drawn brows and the thin line of his lips. A small tic at his jaw caught her attention. And then one corner of his mouth twitched. Right before his lips started a slow curve.

She squinted at him, certain the shadows were playing tricks on her.

White teeth flashed, and then the sound of his laughter filled the small sports car.

Frowning, she shook her head. "You are the strangest man I have ever met," she said, leaning back against her door and away from him. He and his wicked laugh were taking up too much space. He unsettled her, made her crazy. She didn't much like the feeling. She liked her men predictable. Sort of. Besides, he wasn't her man.

"Sweetheart, I'm not the one who wears spoons on my nose." He cleared his throat in an obvious attempt to stop laughing. "Which clashes with your gold earrings, by the way."

"Oh, so now you're a comedian." She twisted around to open her door. "I wouldn't quit my day job if I were you."

He quieted. "I may not have a choice."

She swiveled back to him, wide-eyed, the open car door forgotten. "Are you kidding? Was the ambassador that ticked off?"

"Yes." He paused, and she felt the blood leave her face. "I'm teasing you. I wouldn't admire someone with so little sense of humor."

She snorted indelicately. "You're not funny."

"You were." His slow grin pierced the shadows and made her skin tingle.

"That wasn't my goal, trust me." She sighed. There was no point in explaining herself now. The ambassador wasn't upset. And Jack apparently didn't hate her. She supposed that was enough. Except a small voice still demanded absolution.

"I know." He reached out a hand and trailed the back across her cheek.

Tiny darts of awareness pricked her nerve endings. The tone of his voice had changed. No residual laughter lurked in its quiet timbre. It sounded husky, slightly hoarse, just as it had when they were dancing.

"That was a nice thing you did," he said, his hand moving to the back of her neck. "That woman's date had no sense of humor at all."

"Yeah." Her voice came out a squeak. She didn't care. All she could think about was how warm his palm was pressed to her nape. Her eyes drifted closed, and she took a deep breath before opening them again.

He'd moved his face closer, and with assisted pressure from behind her neck, she leaned forward to accommodate him.

Their lips brushed once briefly, brushed again. It was awkward sitting in this small car, the gearshift sticking up between them, the murky gray shadows hiding their expressions. Although, she didn't think she wanted to see his face. If she did, she'd probably chicken out and not kiss him. Tomorrow she was headed for Switzerland. Starting anything romantic now would be downright foolish. But in the dark, a kiss somehow didn't seem to count.

His mouth was suddenly on hers again, and she parted her lips slightly, half in surprise, half in hunger. Her heart had started pounding so hard she couldn't hear herself think. Not that she could talk herself out of this at the moment. Not when his hand was curved around her neck and he trailed the tip of his tongue across her mouth and...

A string of excited Italian burst into the air outside the car. Dazed, Gina stayed where she was, but Jack pulled back slowly. He let his hand fall away as he turned to see what the commotion was—it had interrupted the promise of a terrific kiss. Regaining her wits, she followed his gaze.

An older couple had just gotten out of a red Fiat two cars away, the woman talking a mile a minute and the man waving her off as he headed for the elevator.

Jack listened for a moment. "A lovers' quarrel," he said.

"A wake-up call," she muttered with a sigh, and got out.

He followed her to the elevator, where they waited in silence for the car to return. She carefully avoided looking at him, and he made no attempt to get her attention. When the doors slid open, he stepped aside and placed a hand at the small of her back...it was bare, sensitive where his flesh met hers. Despite the balmy summer air, goose bumps sprung to the surface, trailing her spine, spanning her waist.

She cleared her throat as if the sudden noise would

erase the telling bumps, then backed herself into a corner of the car. From there she got a good view of his strong profile as he depressed the button to his floor. Then he stepped back under the revealing overhead light, which only served to make him better looking instead of highlighting his flaws. But she supposed he did have some flaws. His jaw, for one, was too square, and the cleft dimpling his chin was slightly off center.

With all the eyeballing she was doing, he made no effort to meet her eyes, she noticed, and wondered if he was already regretting their kiss.

His eyebrows were furrowed a little, his lips slightly pursed, and she got the impression that he was deep in thought. Probably wondering how to gracefully tell her to buzz off.

"What did you mean by wake-up call?" he asked suddenly, and she jumped because his deep, husky voice made him seem nearer.

Gathering her wits, she rolled her eyes toward the ceiling. "You know what I mean. Don't expect me to spell it out."

"I assure you, I don't."

She frowned at the way he was frowning. He really didn't get it. "Well, Jack, we shouldn't have been, uh, smooching."

"Why not?"

She let out a loud, exasperated breath. "Because."

"Good reason." His gaze flicked over her, his expression bland. The doors opened, and he held a safeguarding hand at one side and waited for her to leave the car.

She let his sarcasm set in, but as soon as she got out to the corridor, she turned around, ready for battle. He'd been staring at her butt, but his gaze slowly rose to hers.

Gina forgot what she was going to say.

His face was too close, his masculine scent surrounding her like a silken web, tripping up her thoughts, summoning the goose bumps back. He wasn't playing fair.

"You didn't let me finish," she said abruptly, and backed up a step. "Because...because it isn't a good idea."

He nodded, his expression serious except for the mild amusement glinting in his blue eyes. "That explains everything."

"You're a smart guy. Think about it." She started to back up again, but the hem of her dress got tangled with her strappy evening sandals.

"I have." His gaze held hers. "Half the damn night."

Using the problem with her hem to gratefully break eye contact, she stooped slightly to untangle herself. The blatant intent in his eyes wasn't news. It was foolish to feel so shaky all of a sudden. He'd been telegraphing his interest since well before dinner. And like a smitten teenager, she'd responded.

Except now his purpose seemed more intense, almost predatory, as though he wouldn't think twice about stripping her dress off with his teeth right here in the hall. The prospect both frightened and fascinated her.

She fumbled with her hem, and he laid a hand on her bare arm to help steady her. That had not been part of her plan. She shoved the fabric aside and heard the delicate silk rip.

"Oh, great. Now I owe Greta a dress." She raised reluctant eyes, and at the same time it occurred to her that since the dress was already torn...

At the tempting thought, her cheeks flooded with heat.

His gaze roamed her face, his mouth curving in an enigmatic smile. "I would give just about anything to know what just went through that imaginative little head of yours."

"Fat chance."

"I figured."

Part of her dress was still caught, and she limped the remaining four feet to his apartment. "Are you going to open the door or just stand there?"

"Are those my only options?"

"You got it." She stood in front of his door and rubbed her arm where it had hit the wall when she'd fumbled her untangling efforts, and refused to look at him.

She heard him insert the key into the lock and suffered a pang of disappointment that he'd given up so easily. Of course, the night was still young, and they had the entire apartment to themselves and...

What was she thinking? Nothing was going to happen. Nothing *could* happen. They orbited different planets, and she wasn't into one-night stands.

She reached out to turn the knob, but he stopped her by covering her hand with his.

"The rules have changed, Gina," he whispered, brushing the hair off her jaw as he spoke. "What are we going to do about that?"

His touch was light, silky, almost as if he knew how much more tempting that made his subtle offer.

She held her breath, then released it slowly. He was giving her a chance to think about what could happen once they crossed the threshold. He was being fair, cautious, considerate, but she didn't want him to be, damn it. At least if she did something impulsively she could forestall the regret. Now she'd have to enter the bargain with her eyes open.

She sagged slightly against him. It was hell being a responsible adult.

"I'm not sure how to take that response," he said, his lips taking over for his hands, trailing her jaw, and she smiled at the slip of Jackson's halo. He wasn't playing so fair, after all.

"Do I have to give you an answer?" she asked, even knowing how wimpy that sounded.

"One way or another." He nipped at the corner of her mouth.

She turned her head, giving his lips full access to hers, and she figured that was answer enough.

So did he.

He flattened his palm against the wall near her head, pressed his body against hers and effectively pinned her to the wall. His breathing turned ragged as the tip of his tongue lingered on a path across her lower lip.

This wasn't the Jackson who made certain his shirts were starched just so, or that the kitchen appliances all gleamed as if they were brand new. He seemed slightly out of control, or at least vaguely struggling for some semblance of command.

The knowledge made Gina heady with power and just a little afraid. Or maybe it was the hungry greed that usurped his barely contained composure and fueled his eager mouth that tilted Gina off balance, caused her to fear her own foolish desire to lie down in this man's bed.

If they ever made it to the bedroom...instead of standing here, in the corridor, out in the open for any neighbor to see. When Jackson realized what was happening, he was going to freak.

She opened her mouth a little to point out the wisdom of moving inside, but he took the gesture as an invitation and covered her mouth with his, his tongue doing wonderfully wicked things to hers.

She didn't want to move. Not ever again. She wanted to just stand here with his chest rubbing against her breasts as he deepened the kiss, his arm cradling her cheek as he braced himself against the wall.

He whispered her name with such tender longing that it didn't matter that they were touching nowhere else. They might just as well have been lying naked in each other's arms. The simple utterance created such an incredible intimacy, and revealed like nothing else his unadulterated desire to be with her.

It wasn't her imagination. It couldn't be.

Jackson wanted her with a fierceness that made her pulse race into the next millennium.

Her knees got a little rubbery, and she didn't know how long she could hold out without making a complete fool of herself by sliding to the floor.

As if reading her mind, Jack slid his other arm around her without breaking the kiss and she gladly sank against him, letting him wedge his arm between her and the wall.

She welcomed the increased pressure against her breasts, the hand that rested at the top of her buttocks. She couldn't breathe, doubted she ever would again, but she didn't care. For the moment, it didn't matter that she hadn't lost the five pounds she'd planned on losing before this trip, or that her hairdresser had snipped too much off her bangs. Jackson made her feel beautiful and wanted. And she realized with a small start that after Nick, she sorely needed to feel this way.

His mouth retreated slightly, pressed back against her, then pulled away.

Slowly, she blinked up at him.

A fine sheen of moisture glistened from his wryly slanted lips. "Guess I'm getting a little ahead of myself."

She disagreed. He was hard, his erection still nudging her lower belly as it had from the beginning. She smiled but said nothing.

"You look pretty pleased," he said, brushing a lock of hair away from her face yet keeping hold of the strands, slowly rubbing them between his thumb and forefinger as if mesmerized by their texture. He brought his gaze back to her face. "Does that mean I'm forgiven?"

The lazy yet possessive way his eyes roamed her features undermined his feeble attempt at humility. He wasn't looking for forgiveness. He knew what he'd done to her, and he was confident she'd let him do it again.

"Maybe."

Their gazes locked.

One of his eyebrows rose in inquiry. Before she could answer, he lifted her hand and pressed his lips into the center of her palm.

She already knew he didn't always play fair, but she hadn't realized Jackson was a scrapper. Resisting the urge to snatch back her too sensitive hand, she forced her gaze to remain steady with his.

"What is my forgiveness contingent upon?" he asked, turning her hand over to kiss the back of her knuckles.

"How well you do when it really counts."

She startled a laugh out of him. He studied her

closely, probably waiting for her to blush. "You wouldn't happen to be referring to my performance?"

Gina gave an innocent shrug. She needed a swift kick for goading him. Her provocative statement implied she expected to end up in his bed. She hadn't really decided that yet, had she?

Yeah, right. She smiled, casually, as if her heart weren't doing cartwheels in her chest. "Is that what you think I meant?"

"Without a doubt." He slanted his head and pressed a gentle kiss across her lips. When she started to respond, he retreated. "Care for a sneak preview?"

He lifted a hand to cup her jaw, and she was amazed to discover how large his hands were. She hadn't really noticed before, but now his fingers splayed deep into her hair, massaging her scalp and making pudding of her knees again. Being so tall herself, she seldom met with this experience, and she liked the feminine feel it gave her.

Letting her eyes close, briefly, blissfully, she pressed her cheek more snugly into his palm.

"Gina, you're going to have to make a decision." His voice was even raspier than before, and when she opened her eyes to gaze at him he looked oddly as though he were in some kind of pain. "Are we going inside?" he asked, heat radiating off him like an August noon sun.

"Of course we are," she said…a second before his meaning sunk into her dazed brain. She swallowed. "Yes, we are," she repeated more confidently.

He nodded, lightly touching her cheek one last time, the desire in his eyes briefly softening. "This is going to be so right."

She hoped so, she wanted to believe that, too, and

the fact that he volunteered that opinion made her heart take wings.

Jack gripped the doorknob and suddenly she was impatient with need and longing and undeniable hope.

She wanted to hurry him, yet she wanted to make the moment last. Because his eyes were only for her, and she couldn't remember ever feeling more alive. And truly happy that she was Gina Hart, the kid from Brooklyn.

A silly giggle rose in her throat and spilled from her lips. The corners of his eyes crinkled with amusement as he turned the knob.

"Jackson?"

The concerned feminine voice slipped through the open crack a second before the knob flew out of Jack's hand. He blinked in astonishment and stepped back to look at the petite blonde staring at them in shocked disbelief from inside his doorway.

He exhaled loudly. "Miranda."

Chapter Thirteen

"I must say, you make a striking couple," Miranda said as she lit her second cigarette in five minutes, and eyed them assessingly through the haze of smoke. The cigarette was of the long slender European variety and somehow didn't look so repulsive between her small, dainty fingers. "Why didn't you tell me about her, Jackson?"

Everyone was being so civil it gave Gina the willies. Back home, the last time her neighbor, Val Rigatti, had gotten caught messing with her best friend's fiancé, Val had gotten a full set of curlers ripped from her hair.

He exhaled. "I've only known Gina for three days. She came to the embassy looking for help when her passport and money were stolen. We aren't exactly a couple."

Gina chortled to herself. Miranda was going to have a field day with this opening.

The blonde raised one cool eyebrow and glanced from Jackson to Gina. "Really?"

When silence followed and stretched, disappointment drenched Gina like a sudden rain shower. This woman was too much of a wuss for Jack. She should have been really ticked, ready to scratch his eyes out. Gina's, too.

Instead, she just stood there, not a hair out of place, her eyes a blank blue, looking as though she were at a Junior League meeting instead of facing her two-timing boyfriend.

Gina slid Jack a hostile look. She could tell he didn't like Miranda puffing away in his kitchen, but of course he wasn't in a position to criticize anyone.

Although, to his credit, he hadn't tried to deny anything. Not that he could have. Miranda may not have actually seen anything, but Gina's swollen lips and mussed-up hair spoke volumes.

In fact, Jack didn't look so hot himself. His bow tie was barely intact, his shirt no longer tucked neatly into his cummerbund. His hair had long since lost its usual swept-back style and now fell in two thick locks across his forehead. Basically, he was a mess. That cheered Gina up a little.

"So, how was the dinner?" Miranda asked, and this time when she stubbed out her cigarette, Gina noticed that her hand shook slightly.

Gina's heart constricted. She was to blame, too. She'd known about Miranda. Nothing specific. But there had been enough clues, and deep down she knew there was someone in Jack's life. But she'd chosen to ignore the warning signs because she'd wanted to be with Jack.

Of course, she still didn't know exactly what his and Miranda's relationship was—nothing had been spelled out. Gina only hoped they weren't officially engaged. Somehow, that would make her feel worse than a blood-sucking leech.

"Dinner was—" Jack half smiled as he lounged back against the counter and let his gaze wander over Gina "—interesting."

In spite of herself, Gina's body tensed with awareness at his casual glance, and she gripped the edge of the butcher block island she was leaning against. She automatically looked at Miranda, who watched her with keen and disconcerting interest.

The light was too bright in the kitchen. Why the hell were they standing here, of all places? Gina wanted to go to bed and crawl deep beneath the covers. She'd wanted to do that since the moment Miranda opened the door. But Gina knew she had to stay and take her lumps, face the ugly consequences of being impulsive. That was the only way she could wake up tomorrow and look herself in the mirror without cringing. Besides, she doubted she was still welcome to the guest room tonight.

"I was trying to make it back in time to accompany you," Miranda said, "but I got delayed in London. I knew tonight was important." She concentrated on withdrawing another cigarette from a muted tapestry case, a small smile playing about her lips. "I'm glad you at least didn't have to go alone."

"I'm sorry you cut your holiday short." Jackson picked up her gold monogrammed lighter and flicked a flame to her cigarette. "After this one, can we move to the living room?"

Miranda inhaled while drawing her head back, then shrugged. "I don't plan on staying much longer. I suppose I shouldn't even have convinced Isabella to let me in."

The fact the she didn't have her own key to Jack's apartment as Gina had assumed suddenly filled her with foolish and unwarranted relief.

"Nonsense. I'm glad you did," Jack said, and Miranda's lips curved in a wry smile.

Heck, even Gina knew that despite his outward composure, he wasn't being totally honest. She drummed her fingers on the edge of the butcher block, waiting for someone to say something.

"Me, too," she finally piped in to fill the sudden and awkward silence. "I'm glad I got to meet you. Since I'm headed for Switzerland tomorrow…and there's no telling when I'll stop in Rome again. Not that I would need to go to the embassy again. So I probably wouldn't see either of you, anyway…."

Gina met Miranda's amused gaze and stopped her babbling.

Silence was not a bad thing, after all.

Gina wished she'd learn when to shut up.

"Are you on holiday?" Miranda asked with polite but definite interest, and amazingly, no evidence of malice.

Mentally, Gina kicked herself. So far she'd been able to stay out of the conversation. Now she'd opened herself up. "I wish. I'm a courier, and hopefully there'll still be a package waiting for me in Zurich."

She said the remark teasingly and glanced at the calendar on her watch, mostly for something to do. She stared hard, swallowed harder. "Is tomorrow really the tenth?" she asked.

Jack was nodding when she dragged her panicked gaze away from her watch. She was in trouble.

Gina straightened and took a deep breath. "Jack, I need my passport. I have to get to Switzerland tomorrow."

"Relax," he said, frowning. "Greta says she has your passport ready and—"

"Don't tell me to relax, damn it." Vaguely, Gina saw Miranda's head turn sharply in her direction, but Gina was too upset to care what the woman was thinking right now. "I have to pick up that package by tomorrow at noon or lose the best customer I have."

"Okay." Jack put out a hand. "Just calm down—"

"Look, Bucko, you may be able to afford to blow off a few hundred bucks, but I can't. Got it?" She pushed a hand through her hair. Where had the time gone? One minute she had a couple of days to kill, and then, poof. This was bad. Very bad. This particular client accepted no excuses. "Jack, *you* know I'm no hooker. Surely you can vouch for me until the police do whatever it is they have to do."

Miranda's intake of breath was audible even from where Gina stood. "This is getting more interesting by the minute," she said, and leaned back to draw on her cigarette.

Jack ignored her. "Possibly," he told Gina. "But if you leave tomorrow, you'll only have to come back."

"Not *if*, Jack. I *am* leaving tomorrow." Gina started to pace, then realized she didn't have enough room. She had to talk to Greta. Maybe it wasn't too late to call. Without her passport, Gina was sunk.

"Jack?" Miranda's face creased. "When did you start going by Jack?"

He glanced absently at Miranda, then centered a stern frown on Gina. "I don't like that look on your face," he said, his tone a warning. "Don't do anything stupid."

Gina folded her arms across her chest. Simmering anger bubbled dangerously close to the surface. Probably more anger than was warranted. But her nerves were stretched thin. "How quickly you forget that *I'm* the victim here."

"Would you two tell me what's going—" Miranda

cut herself off and put up one hand. "On second thought, I don't want to know." She gathered up her cigarettes and lighter, and stuffed them into her brown designer purse.

Then she raised herself on tiptoe and lightly bussed Jack's cheek. He stared at her as though he'd forgotten she was there.

Miranda sighed. "I'll talk to you tomorrow." She arched her eyebrows in Gina's direction, her expression speculative. "Or maybe later in the week. Looks like you have your hands full for now."

Jack's cheeks puffed out as he exhaled. He regarded Miranda for a long, distracted moment before saying, "I'll walk you to your car."

"Not necessary. Your doorman parked it for me."

"You still have to get there."

She held up a silencing hand. "He'll bring it to the door."

"Miranda..."

"I'm tired, Jackson," she said, her eyes meeting his with a private message. "Don't push."

He nodded, looking weary himself. "I'll call tomorrow."

By way of saying goodbye, Miranda smiled at Gina before she left the kitchen. Gina's anger lapsed, and she stood dumbfounded until she heard the front door click.

What was the deal with these people? Were they always this disgustingly civilized? Miranda had hardly asked any questions, much less raised her voice even once. She hadn't even demanded the answer to the obvious question, like where was Gina staying.

She turned abruptly to Jack. "So, I got to meet the illusive Miranda, after all." A slow self-deprecating expression spread across his face and fueled her smugness.

"She seems like a nice lady. When's the date, Jackson?"

He didn't pretend to misunderstand. It would have grossly irritated her if he had. He simply studied her in brief silence before he said, "It's not what you think. Miranda truly is just a friend."

"Have you ever slept with her?" Gina gasped, horrified those words had come out of her mouth. "You're right. It's none of my business. Now, about my passport—"

"I'll answer your question. I have nothing to hide."

"I'd rather you tell me about my passport." Her heart pounded wildly. If he didn't let her change the subject, she was never going to forgive him. She didn't want to know if he'd ever slept with Miranda. She didn't care. She couldn't care. The answer would crush her.

He let out a loud sigh. "I don't know anything more than you do about your passport."

He'd given up too easily. He'd slept with her, all right. Gina lifted her chin. "Can we call Greta?"

"It's midnight, Gina."

"Oh."

"Miranda and I are not engaged, nor have we ever been." He held up a hand when she started to protest the unwanted information. And when that didn't stop her, he reached out and grabbed her by the shoulders, surprising her into clamping her mouth shut. "We are friends. Have we ever talked about getting married? Yes. Seriously? No."

At his brief pause, she started to remind him she hadn't asked, didn't want to know, but before she could, he added, "And if we ever did get married, it would be because it made sense."

She frowned, tensing under his touch. "What do you mean, made sense?"

He loosened his grip, looking oddly wary as his gaze held hers. Slowly, deliberately, he said, "She'd be the perfect diplomat's wife. And in return, Miranda would have a comfortable, well-stationed life."

His matter-of-fact tone chilled her almost as much as his words. "Oh, I see. Sure, that makes perfect sense."

Obviously she'd done an admirable job of concealing her sarcasm, because his gaze dropped to her lips and he looked as though he wanted to kiss her.

She tried to shake loose of his hold, but he wouldn't have it. He drew her a fraction closer and said, "That's strictly in theory, of course."

"Of course." It didn't matter. Gina wasn't about to play second fiddle. Besides, it was no secret she could never be a candidate for a diplomat's wife. Not that she was interested.

She thought it might be too late in life to be developing allergies or a sinus problem, but something was causing the pressure to build up around her eyes, and all she could think of was getting to her room and lying down.

Just as he lowered his head, she pulled free, jerking away. "It's late," she said, rubbing the chill out of her arms and stepping back. "And I have a big day tomorrow."

The reminder that she was leaving was deliberate, and she knew he got the message by the sudden set of his jaw, the slight creasing of his forehead. She didn't wait for him to say anything. She grabbed her purse off the butcher block island.

Out of the corner of her eye, she saw Jack lounge against the counter, making no move to go after her.

Not that she wanted him to.

Of course she didn't.

She'd made it to the door when he called her name, and against her will, she hesitated, without turning around.

"Just for the record," he said. "I've never slept with Miranda."

JACKSON FINALLY GAVE UP trying to get to sleep around three. Tempted to throw back a snifter of brandy or two, he settled for a glass of milk, instead. Isabella didn't buy milk often since he drank it so rarely, and with the first sip he made a face when he realized that it was a low-fat version. Obviously this had been bought with Gina in mind.

He smiled, pushing the glass aside and thinking about how Gina always questioned the fat content in everything she ate, but wolfed down chocolate as though all the Swiss factories were shutting down tomorrow.

Sitting in the semidark living room, he absently rubbed his bare chest. He didn't want her to leave. Of course she would. She had a life. It was asinine to think she'd hang around Rome for no reason. She sure as hell wasn't going to stick around for him. He'd been a first-class jerk tonight.

He should have explained about Miranda when he'd had the opportunity earlier. Except what was he supposed to have said? They were just friends, period. Did he have to provide Gina with an inventory of his friends, for God's sake?

Oh, hell.

He closed his eyes and pinched the bridge of his nose. Miranda should have been explained. Pure and simple. In most people's eyes, their relationship was a little more than casual, even if he and Miranda knew differently. Gina had the right to know that at least.

Maybe.

He stared moodily out the window at a distant street lamp. So far, all he'd done was kiss Gina. Did that give her the right to a history of his love life?

Muttering a colorful oath, he shifted in the hundred-year-old chair. The damn thing wasn't even comfortable. He briefly wondered if it had been more inviting when he was a kid but had since deteriorated. But he couldn't remember ever being permitted to sit on this particular chair. It had belonged to part of a group in his parents' sitting room where he'd never been allowed.

Actually, no one ever used that room.

He laughed suddenly. Perhaps his mother hadn't been the stuffed shirt he'd thought. Maybe she hadn't been protective of the furniture. She simply knew the chairs weren't comfortable.

And here he was, like a damn fool, working his tail off to reclaim them.

The thought struck him as absurdly funny and he laughed harder.

A dark figure appeared near the dining room and he swiped at his eyes, figuring the shadows from the street lamp were playing tricks on him.

"Jackson?"

Gina's voice sounded tentative, just a little frightened.

"Yeah." He straightened, straining his eyes to get a clearer picture of her. "It's me."

"You startled me," she said, and when she stepped closer, he saw that she had a hand to her throat. "I couldn't sleep, and I was just going to the kitchen for some milk...what are you doing out here in the dark?''

He watched her wrap her arms around herself. Whatever she was wearing was short, ending at about mid-thigh. He raised his gaze to her shadowed face. No sense torturing himself. "Sitting here thinking about what a mess I made of things tonight."

She responded with silence and, for a moment, remained completely still. Then she drew one hand up and down her opposite arm. "Do you mind if I get some milk?"

"You don't have to ask permission, Gina. You know you're free to do whatever you like here."

She stopped and appeared to stiffen. "I'm a guest...a very grateful guest. I don't want you to think I take anything you've done for me for granted."

He reached for a lamp and flicked the switch. Light flooded the room, and she blinked rapidly at the intrusion. It wasn't a bright illumination, more a soft yellowish glow, but it clearly startled her, and she crossed her arms over her chest.

"Tonight is very likely your last night here, and I don't want us to part on bad terms tomorrow."

"It had better be my last night, and if you don't hurry up and turn off that light, bad terms hell, I'll never speak to you again."

He tried not to look, or at least not be too obvious about it, but he couldn't help feasting on the sight of long bare legs and the curve of one hip outlined by her sheer peach nightie. Unfortunately, her crossed arms hid a bounty he could only imagine. However, he'd already seen enough from her dress tonight to imagine plenty, and his body tightened with a familiar longing that was beginning to threaten his sanity.

"I want to talk," he said.

She took a step back. "Not with the light on."

"Okay." He quickly flipped the switch, afraid she'd retreat, and the room once again was plunged into darkness.

Because his eyes had briefly grown accustomed to the light, the place seemed even darker now, but it didn't matter. He'd already seen enough to make his body hum with excitement. And ironically, although he truly had wanted to talk, he now had about as much ability to concentrate as a kid trying to do homework in front of the television.

"I'll be right back," she said. "I need to get something from my room."

"You look fine the way you are." He almost choked on the word *fine*.

"Right."

"I was trying to be diplomatic. Would begging work?"

Her answering silence almost convinced him he'd just blown it again, then she laughed, too. "This isn't like you, Jack."

"You know me that well?" he asked, the patronizing lilt to her voice annoying him.

"I think so."

"Must be reassuring to be so confident."

"You should talk."

He frowned, not understanding. "Are we reverting to our conversation the night I bailed you out of jail?"

"You're the one who jumped to conclusions."

He was sorry she was still smarting about the incident, especially since her version wasn't totally accurate, but he wasn't about to split hairs. Instead, he asked,

"If you're deliberately trying to start an argument, I'd prefer to discuss what's really bothering you."

She sighed, and he wished the light was on. He wanted to see her face, study any nuance in her expression that would tell him he was pushing too hard.

"You should have told me about Miranda," she said, and he reconsidered, suddenly glad the room was shadowed so she couldn't see the wry smile that came unbidden to his lips.

Knowing it was worthless to point out that he'd already tried explaining, he simply said, "You're right. I had the opportunity at dinner and I ignored it."

"*Avoid* would be a better word choice here, Jack."

"Wait a minute. That's not true. Earlier I didn't think it was necessary. I didn't know we were going to end up—"

"Yes, you did."

Accustomed once again to the darkness, he stared at her shadowy silhouette, tempted to shock her out of her smugness by flipping on the light. Hell, she didn't let him get away with a damn thing.

"You did know," she insisted again, "and you also knew that I was…interested." She cleared her throat. "Very interested. But I wouldn't have been if I had known about your relationship with Miranda. I could have made a big mistake. One we would both have had to live with."

"You're telling me you would have slept with me tonight."

Even in the darkness, he could tell his bluntness had startled her. Her head jerked, and she was rubbing her arms again. "Maybe."

"Then I assume that in order to arrive at that kind

of decision there is something about me that attracted you and—"

Interrupting him, she said, "Fishing for compliments?"

"You know better," he answered calmly, understanding that she still smarted. "I'm only trying to say that I would hope respect had something to do with your attraction. Operating on that assumption, why can't you believe me now when I tell you there is nothing romantically linking Miranda and me?"

Gina shifted, and for a moment he thought she was leaving, but she moved farther into the room and sat in a chair closer to him.

With her positioned in this new location, light filtered in at just the right angle, enabling him to see her face more clearly, and the earnest look that softened her eyes and parted her lips ever so slightly tore at his gut.

Of course, the filtered lighting was still murky enough that he could be imagining her expression, seeing what he hoped to find. Except he wasn't the type given to such fanciful thinking.

"You're right," she said, speaking slowly, as if trying to choose her words carefully. "I do admire and respect you. I like that you're not some prima donna and that you jump in and help wherever needed. I like the way you treat Isabella and Marcy, who both have such wonderful things to say about you that—"

"Okay, okay." Embarrassed, he put up a silencing hand.

She laughed softly. "No problem. I've run out of your good points."

Jackson chuckled along with her, then sobered. "You missed one. I don't deceive people."

After a brief silence she said, "I really hate that

you're so logical. That is not one of your strong suits in my book." Gina paused again. "But you're right and I do believe you. And I was wrong in assuming that you and Miranda were...well, that tonight you were just doing a little slumming on the side."

His eyebrows drew together in confusion. "Slumming?" Then her meaning hit him, rocketing anger through him faster than a mirror reflected light. "What are you saying, Gina?"

At his abrupt tone, her chin lifted. "Lighten up, Jack. That's just an expression."

"Meaning?"

She ran a hand through her tousled hair. "It doesn't matter."

He should let it go. The subject was making her uncomfortable. "Stop putting yourself down, Gina."

Her surprise filled the air with silence, then she snorted. "Is that what you think I was doing? For heaven's sake, Jack, why would I do that?"

Her tone was dismissive, slightly amused, but he wasn't fooled. Body language was far more telling, and the way she sat rigidly in her chair and hugged herself belied her words.

"You really are arrogant, Jackson," she said, her poise clearly slipping as her voice rose an octave. "Why you think I would worry about fitting in with that hoity-toity bunch of air-kissing, hot-air blowers is—"

"Gina?"

She sputtered to a halt and took a deep breath. He knew she didn't mean what she was saying, and she'd regret the unkind words as soon as she calmed down.

"I was proud of you tonight," he said quietly. "I was proud to be with you."

"Proud—?" Her voice caught, but startled disbelief quickly turned to skepticism. "Why?"

He smiled. "Fishing for compliments?"

She ignored his teasing. "I embarrassed you, Jack. I didn't mean to, but I did, and I appreciate your being a good sport but—"

"I'm sick and tired of you thinking you have everything all figured out," he said, noting she had straightened as if ready for flight. "Especially when you're wrong," he added flatly, and when she started to argue, he said, "Shut up. I'm not finished."

Growling low in her throat, she sank back and crossed her arms. "This chair isn't very comfortable, so make it snappy."

"Look, I already told you I think it was a nice thing you did for that woman and her spoon trick. I didn't say it to hear myself talk. I meant it. You were concerned about poaching on what you perceived was another woman's territory, and although you were wrong, I admire that you have those boundaries."

She stirred and he held up a hand. "You have been kind and non-assuming toward Isabella, who has smiled more in the past three days than she has all year. And if you don't quit squirming, I'm going to go on for another ten minutes."

"Jackson." Her voice was pleading and a little strangled as she struggled to her feet.

"Okay, okay. I have just one question."

She stopped, sitting tentatively at the edge of her seat.

"You said earlier that you had been...interested." Shadows fell across her face, but he saw her wary eyes clearly. "Are you still?"

She hesitated long enough for him to get his answer, and he rose from the chair.

Chapter Fourteen

Gina watched Jack come to her through the darkness. His movements were slow, deliberate, almost like a tiger stalking his prey, and excitement rippled down her spine, causing a slickness between her thighs.

An outside street lamp shone in from behind him, making a view of his face impossible. Carefully, she kept her expression hidden in the shadow of his body to even the score. She wasn't sure what he'd find revealed in her eyes. Fear. Excitement. Longing.

Foolish hope.

She swallowed and rose to meet him, reminding herself that this meant nothing more than one night. That's all he was offering. That's all she wanted.

Jack was shirtless, and when he clamped his hands around her wrists and gently pulled her toward him, she offered no resistance, eagerly letting her palms hone in on his soft black chest hairs, his hardening nipples.

She wished she could see him more clearly, allow her eyes to feast on the taut muscle she felt beneath her fingers. But more light would give him the same advantage, and she wasn't quite ready to share the tiny dimples at the backs of her thighs that no amount of exercise seemed to eliminate.

"Gina?" Releasing her wrists, he moved his hands down her back, lingering at the curve of her buttocks.

She tilted her head back to look up at him, the light shining fully in her eyes. Quickly, she ducked her head.

He slipped a finger under her chin and forced her gaze to his. She missed the feel of his arm around her and snuggled closer. Beneath his silk pajama bottoms, he was rock hard already. Excitement shimmied across her shoulders.

His mouth descended on hers, but his kiss was brief and frustratingly unsatisfying. "Gina? Let's go to my room."

She thought about demanding a better kiss before she agreed.

One corner of Jack's mouth lifted. "What's that sly grin for?"

She pressed her palms harder against his aroused nipples. "Kiss me and I'll tell you."

His hands moved against her back, and then they were cupping her elbows and he forced her hands higher until they were around his neck.

"Sensitive?" she asked innocently.

Without warning, he slipped his hands beneath her top and filled his palms with her naked breasts.

She gasped.

He smiled. "I figured I could show you easier than explain," he said, slowly kneading and massaging. "It sort of felt like this."

She closed her eyes and fought to stay conscious. His touch made her both hot and cold and more than a little faint. Her arms grew slack and the starch left her knees.

"Now might be a good time to head for my bed," he whispered close to her ear, his breath tickling her skin an instant before his tongue blazed a path across her jaw to her mouth.

"Why didn't you say so?" she grumbled, and he laughed while continuing to nibble and taste, backing her out of the living room, bumping into two walls before they found the hall.

It should have been a clear and easy shot to his room at the end of the hallway, but they managed to run into the wall twice again and the doorjamb to her room once while he continued to kiss her and take wild nips at her breasts through her baby doll top.

His unbridled enthusiasm both surprised and excited her, and she knew this was not likely to be a night she'd forget for a long time. But she would eventually. She'd have to. That was part of their unspoken deal.

As soon as they made it through his door, he reached for the light switch and even managed to flick on a lamp before she tugged at his hand.

"Let's not have the lights on," she said, and tried to convince him not to argue by sprinkling the corner of his mouth with tiny, rapid kisses.

He kissed her back, hard, then said, "Why?"

"Because."

"I need a better reason," he said, his heated gaze lowering to her chest where, in the light, the fabric was so sheer and damp she may as well have been naked. He lifted the hem, then skimmed her waist, cupped her breast.

Gina was torn between sighing with pleasure and screaming at him. She wanted their one-and-only night to be perfect. That's what she wanted him to remember. Not that her hips were a little too wide, or that the stubborn beginnings of cellulite dimpled the backs of her thighs. Yet what was she supposed to do? Admit she looked better in her clothes? Or in the dark?

She shifted away from his touch, the pleasure of his nearness dwindling a little.

His gaze found and held hers. "Having second thoughts?" he whispered, and the dread on his face made her lips curve.

She shook her head. "I just don't want the light on."

"Okay." He nodded, but looked totally confused as he reached for the switch again. "How about a couple of candles?"

It wasn't fair that one of his hands had returned to caress her breast, and the other was molded to the curve of her rear end, pressing her against his erection. It was impossible to think clearly....

"Umm, candles?"

"Only two." He gently bit one of her lobes.

"What's wrong with the dark?"

"I can't see you."

"So, you know where everything is."

He stopped nibbling, pulled back and laughed, and she was darn glad it was too dark for them to see each other's faces.

Heat surged to hers. "I didn't mean it like that."

"If I didn't know better, I'd think you were shy." He ran the tip of one finger down her spine, then, slanting his head, kissed the side of her neck.

"Okay, two candles."

"Right."

She ran her palms down his back until three of her fingers became lodged in the elastic waistband of his silk pajamas, which were now riding low after their shuffle to the bedroom. Slowly splaying her fingers, she pressed her palms to his warm flesh. He was taut and solid beneath her touch, his skin sloping over hard muscle, and suddenly she wanted to be able to see him, too.

"Go get the candles," she pleaded.

At her eagerness, he laughed softly. "Yes, ma'am." But he took his time kissing her again, cradling her face in his hands, holding her in place to give his tongue better access.

When they broke away, she shoved him toward the door. As soon as he was gone, she jerked off her baby dolls so fast she heard a small tear, flipped on the light, then dashed for the king-size bed and slid in between the royal blue sheets.

She had the blue-and-gold comforter drawn up under her chin when he returned.

He stopped in the doorway and frowned, his gaze running over her covered form, then drawing to the lamp. "I'm glad to see you've changed your mind about the light."

He had a great chest. Not too much hair, yet not too little, either. And obviously all those rich embassy dinners didn't affect his weight. His stomach was flat with even a hint of ridged muscle, as if he worked at it in some way. His burgundy pajama bottoms rode low on his hips, and the silky material did nothing to hide his slightly aroused state.

Her breath caught and she realized she was staring. "I haven't," she said quickly. "I was just giving you some light to get the candles situated."

"I see." Something near the foot of the bed caught his attention. Amusement flitted across his face before he turned to set the candles on a mahogany table near the armoire.

Her clothes.

He struck a match and an orange flame danced to

life, instantly transforming both candles to minitorches. For a moment he stared at the fire as if transfixed, and Gina pulled the comforter more snugly around her. She felt exposed, vulnerable suddenly. Maybe he was having a change of heart.

Jack turned to her and smiled. "It's almost dawn. In another hour we won't even need them."

"Dawn?" She widened her eyes at the crystal clock sitting on the table beside the bed. They didn't have much time.

As if he'd read her mind, he approached the bed, turned back the comforter on his side, then pulled the drawstrings to his bottoms.

Gina told herself not to stare. If the situation were reversed she'd be so upset and clumsy under his scrutiny, she'd end up totally ruining the mood. But Jack didn't seem at all self-conscious, and when he lowered his bottoms and kicked them aside, she understood why.

He was magnificent. He had runner's thighs, not an ounce of spare fat or skin, but not too muscular. And she already knew about his taut stomach and the way his chest contoured perfectly to her palms. His semi-aroused state made her tingle with anticipation.

Just as he was about to slip into bed with her, she said, "The lamp?" Then shamelessly watched his rear view as he turned to flip the switch.

She would have strangled him if he'd pulled that stunt on her, but then again, he didn't have any flaws to worry about. Just like the rest of him, his rear end was perfect.

"Anything else?" he asked, one eyebrow lifted in amusement as he returned to the bed.

She saw him a little too clearly and thought about

asking him to blow out one of the candles. "Your side's getting cold," she said.

"I expected you to warm it up." In one fluid movement, he slipped between the sheets and pulled her to him, wrapping his arms around her until her breasts flattened against his chest.

"I don't think that's going to be a problem," she said, too breathless to laugh along with him.

He leaned back slightly to look at her, while pushing the hair away from her face. Already she could feel his erection gaining momentum, nudging her belly, making her moist.

"I wish we had more time," he whispered.

She shook her head. "Let's not start second-guessing or wishing or—"

He forced her chin up with the pad of his thumb, and his probing gaze held her suddenly fearful one. "Are you okay with this?"

She blinked, hoping to dispel any baseless doubts or fears. She knew the score. It wasn't as if she were entering into this liaison blindly. Except something had happened tonight. Something both wonderful and horrible.

Gina had fallen in love with Jackson. It had happened the moment he'd understood why she'd had to rescue Brigitte.

"I'm more than okay with this, Jack," she said, lifting her face for his kiss. "I want you to stop talking and show me how an uptight diplomat earns his keep."

She startled a laugh out of him right before he silenced them both by capturing her mouth with his, making a slave of her will as he did deliciously wicked things with his tongue.

When she tried to loop her arms around his neck, he

grabbed both her wrists in one hand, and holding them above her head, he lowered his mouth to her breasts. Cupping first one and then the other with his free hand, he laved the blossoming peaks with his tongue, twirling and nibbling until she was mindless with need.

She tried to shake free of his hold, and he started to oblige her until he realized her intention was to give him equal pleasure. But he wouldn't have that. Instead, his lovemaking grew more untamed, more desperate as he kept her hands securely out of reach while his mouth and fingers drove her near the edge.

He whispered her name over and over, and she remained stubbornly silent for fear something irreversible would slip out. And when he finally poised himself between her thighs and entered her with such exquisite gentleness, Gina knew it was too late. Something irreversible had already happened, and she would never be the same.

GINA SNIFFED THE AIR. She tried to open her eyes to see what that sweet-smelling fragrance was, but prying her eyes open seemed like far too much trouble at the moment.

She yawned, rolled over onto her side and slowly allowed the light to seep into tiny slits between her lashes. Something tickled her nose. She sneezed and her eyes flew open.

She stared at the now familiar French provincial dresser, then blinked. She was in her room. Jack's guest room. She bolted to a sitting position. The sheets fell away from her breasts. Bare breasts.

Quickly, she lifted the sheets. She didn't have a stitch on. How had she...?

Oh, God. She sank back into the pillows with a loud

groan. If Jack had carried her in here, she was never going to speak to him again.

Of course, he couldn't have. She was too tall, and heavy and...

Where was he? She picked her watch up off the cherry nightstand. She groaned again. It was ten-thirty. No wonder he'd brought her back to her room. Isabella had already been here for an hour. She started to yank back the covers, and a rainbow of pink and yellow flower petals sprayed the air.

Startled, she froze, then saw the large arrangement of roses and carnations and mums sitting on the opposite bedside table. Between the pillows and deeper into the cream-colored sheets were a scattering of more petals.

She smiled and reached for the small envelope sitting beside the gold-etched white porcelain vase. The card simply read *Thank you,* and it was signed *Love, Jack.* Her heart started to pump wildly when she read the love part. Although she knew it meant nothing. It was a common sign-off. Probably written absentmindedly. Although, Jack was more precise than to do or say something off the cuff. Plus, he'd signed it ''Jack.''

She reread the few words and frowned. What did he mean by thank you? An appalling thought flitted through her head.

No, not Jack. This had nothing to do with sex. That would be cruel. After all, he'd been considerate enough to make sure she woke up in her own room and didn't have to face Isabella's inquiring eyes.

She scrambled out of bed and searched for something to put on that would get her to the bathroom. Of course, Jack could have brought her to her room for a more self-serving reason. He wouldn't want anyone to know he'd been slumming, either.

Disgusted with her turn of thoughts, Gina pulled on a T-shirt and pair of shorts. He hadn't been slumming. He hadn't. Gina was every bit as...

She was amazed to feel the sting of tears fill her eyes. Shaking her head, she blinked them away. She wasn't going to do this, beat herself up for not being someone she wasn't, or get caught up in the "but only if" game. She had more important things to worry about than analyzing Jack and his motives. Or worrying about how she could fit into his life. It was simple. She couldn't. Last night was last night, and today she had a plane to catch.

SMILING, ISABELLA TURNED away from the stove as Gina entered the kitchen. "Signore Covington said you would be a-sleeping late and that I should save breakfast for you. Come, *cara mia,* I have a nice frittata for you."

Gina's gaze fastened on a bouquet of flowers sitting on the counter. "Yeah, well Signore Covington had no business letting me sleep late. He knows I have to get out of here today."

At her curt tone, Isabella's eyes widened. "He wanted you to rest."

Shame cramped Gina's shoulders and she shrugged sheepishly. "I know. Where did you get the flowers?"

"Signore Covington." Isabella beamed, and then a worried frown puckered her bushy eyebrows. "Some arrived for you, too. Signore Covington...he was going to a-put them in your room." She wagged a finger. "I told him that was not a-proper."

Gina hid a smile at the woman's inquisitive gaze, but said nothing. The housekeeper would find out soon enough that Jack had not heeded her warning. "That was very nice of him, wasn't it?" Gina said idly, wondering what had brought this on. She felt bad for the streak of envy that wove through her. Petty as it was, she sort of wished she alone had received flowers from Jack. Of course, Isabella deserved them, too.

The other woman lifted her slim shoulders. "He is a good, kind man. But he does not think of flowers by himself." She eyed Gina speculatively as she dragged her palms down her starched white apron, then moved the frying pan from the back burner to the front. "He will miss you, *cara mia*. Very much."

Gina inwardly cursed the burst of hope and excitement that Isabella's sincerity sparked. There were plenty of unsentimental reasons why Jack would miss her—like having to go alone to dinner, for one thing, or...

The housekeeper glanced furtively over her shoulder, her eyes lighting with the excitement of imparting a secret. "I think he sent flowers to Signorina Morgan and his secretary, too."

Gina blinked. She was glad the woman had turned back to the stove so she wouldn't question the disappointment that Gina was finding impossible to stuff down. Had all his staff received flowers today?

That hurt.

Well, she wasn't one of his employees. Damn it.

She swallowed, struggling for reason. The man who'd held her in his arms until dawn would not be treating her this way. The flowers had to have been ordered yesterday, she told herself, since they had arrived so early. Of course, someone like Jackson probably could get anything accomplished at the last minute.

It didn't matter.

Gina realized she'd been wringing her hands and had to pry them apart. She didn't want to think about leaving. She had to just do it. Get on the plane and not look back.

She touched Isabella's arm and the older woman turned to look at her. Gina took both her hands, and ducking her head to meet her at eye level, she gave her a sad smile. "You have been so good to me. Will you forgive me if I don't eat?"

Isabella's dark brows came together, and she made a clucking noise with her tongue. "You must eat something."

"I'm in a hurry. But I promise to grab a sandwich at the airport."

The housekeeper patted her hand, her black eyes growing sad. "You will visit?"

Gina didn't want to lie. But what could she say? That she couldn't bear to see Jackson again. That she couldn't survive the day she'd eventually find out he'd married Miranda.

As much as Gina hated to admit it, Miranda was perfect for him. She walked the walk, and talked the talk. Even her blond hair was perfect. And in no time she'd give Jackson two-point-five politically correct children who went to boarding school to learn the queen's English. God forbid a Brooklyn twang should enter the mix.

About to practice a little diplomacy herself, Gina opened her mouth to answer Isabella when the doorbell chimed and the housekeeper's anxious frown turned to a smile.

"Good. It is here. You can see it before you leave," she said, already breaking away to answer the door. Over her shoulder, she added, "The frittata, it will not take so long to eat."

Gina had no idea what Isabella was talking about,

and although she was mildly curious as to what had just arrived, she wasn't interested enough to stick around. As soon as the housekeeper disappeared, Gina hurried to her room and dragged out the two bags she'd hastily repacked. She left them in the foyer when she remembered she hadn't yet arranged for a cab, then set her bouquet of flowers atop them. She had no idea how she was going to manage getting everything on the plane, but she had no intention of leaving her flowers behind.

Isabella apparently heard her and called to her from the living room. As Gina walked toward her, she dabbed at her eyes. They'd grown a little damp. Probably pollen or something.

Near the bay window where there had been a bare space, an antique chair that resembled one of the others near the sofa sat amid layers of brown paper wrapping. Isabella was still tearing bubble wrap away from the legs when Gina approached.

"Signore Covington will be so pleased," she said, looking up to smile at Gina. "Now only three pieces are left."

Gina looked again at the other similar chair. "What do you mean, three pieces left?"

"To find." Isabella waved a bony hand through the air in frustration as if the English word escaped her. "To buy."

Bewildered, Gina shook her head. "Why would he—? I assumed these things belonged to his family."

"*Sì.*" Isabella's expression turned uncharacteristically guarded and she hesitated, averting her gaze and rubbing the fine wood of the chair with her apron.

Gina watched as the woman's struggle to make a decision played out across her face. Her mouth had turned

down at the corners and she looked genuinely dis
tressed.

"Don't tell me," Gina said suddenly, although she
was dying to know now more than ever. She glanced
at her wristwatch. "I'm late, anyway."

"Signore Covington, he is sending a car for you."
Isabella released her apron and raised a wagging finger
in the air. "I'm a-going to tell you something, but you
are a-going to tell no one. Okay?"

Gina knew she should refuse to hear this. Instinct told
her that no good would come of whatever it was Isa
bella was about to reveal. "Okay," she said, and moved
in closer as if to confirm the secret would be safe with
her.

Chapter Fifteen

Jackson peered out his office window as Gina's car pulled up. He watched her get out and walk toward the embassy and wondered if the fact that she had no luggage with her was a good sign. He didn't want her to leave. Yet he had no right to stop her.

Quickly he left the window and returned to his desk. She'd be upstairs in no time. He'd left word with the *carabinieri* to allow her immediate entrance, as unnecessary as that probably had been. By now he figured she had the embassy police wrapped around her little finger.

Papers and file folders were stacked on three corners of his desk because his overburdened in-box could no longer accommodate his shameful neglect. He had barely touched his mail in the past two days, and even a collection of phone messages was beginning to accumulate. He felt the worst about the unreturned calls. The lack of response was rude, unprofessional and unlike him. As a result he'd spent part of his morning remedying the situation. The rest of the time, he'd spent thinking about Gina.

It had taken every ounce of willpower he'd had to get out of bed this morning and return her to her room.

And truthfully, if it hadn't been for Isabella's imminent arrival, he doubted he would have had the moral where withal to have met his obligations.

He wanted Gina. He wanted to see her, touch her smell her. He wanted to hear her laugh, he wanted to watch her make other people smile. He wanted her with such blinding need that it scared the hell out of him.

Jackson stared at the mounting paperwork that would undoubtedly keep him here until midnight. Last week he wouldn't have minded. A mocking smile lifted his lips. Last week he wouldn't have been in this mess. He would have been in control, done what he always had Taken care of business at all costs.

Now he had this insane obsession to be with Gina.

He muttered a vicious curse that also was totally un like him.

It was good she was leaving today. He didn't know her. And what he did know of her made her a totally unsuitable companion for him. Sure, she'd charmed his peers at dinner, although he suspected some of the men were more enthralled by her dress selections.

Was that his problem? Was this simply such a strong physical attraction that it caused his good sense to fly out the window? He was well past the age of letting testosterone do his thinking, but what else could account for this crazy desire to lay Gina across his desk every time she walked into his office?

Or to want to simply sit and watch her sleep for hours?

And when the hell had he developed a taste for Come and Get Me Pink?

He'd thought he'd had it bad yesterday afternoon. Now, after last night, the situation was beginning to seem hopeless. No matter. This had to stop. Right now

Period. In a couple of hours she'd be sitting on a plane to Switzerland. And everything would be back to normal. Including his damned screwy hormones.

A knock at the door had him shuffling papers in an attempt to look busy. Usually Gina opened the door the same time she knocked, then breezed in without hesitation. This time she waited for him to call out an acknowledgment, which drove a dagger of uneasiness into his gut.

She popped her head in, allowed her gaze to briefly meet his, before sweeping the room. "Hi."

"Come on in," he said, setting aside a file. "There's no one here."

Wearing another one of those short skirts he'd come to look forward to, she walked toward the sofa where she usually sat, but stopped halfway there, turned and asked, "Is my passport ready?"

Her question startled him. "Yes, I have it right here." He made no move to retrieve it from his middle drawer. He only stared at her in surprise. After last night, was that the first thing she had to say to him?

She lowered sheepish eyes. "Thanks for the flowers."

He nodded, then rubbed the side of his neck and exhaled a noisy, exasperated sigh. "Look, Gina—"

"About last—" She spoke at the same time he did. "Go ahead," she said, giving him a brief, impersonal smile.

He didn't like the way she was acting, as though last night had been a mistake. "Aren't you going to sit down?"

She made a show of glancing at her watch. "I really should head for the airport. I may have to fly standby on such short notice."

"I had Marcy book you a flight. It leaves in three hours."

"Oh." She blinked, and something that seemed like disappointment shadowed her face and made his chest constrict in an incredibly foolish manner. "Thank you."

It wasn't a heartfelt thanks, and Jackson took that as a further sign she wasn't quite as anxious to leave as she pretended. Maybe she was waiting for him to ask her to stay. Is that what she wanted? Did he?

"We have to talk about last night," he said.

"Yeah, I suppose we do." She sank to the sofa and made a face. "How did I get to my room?"

That wasn't what he had in mind. "I carried you."

She cringed. "You didn't turn the light on, did you?"

"I don't remember. What's this about?"

She sighed, and this time when her eyes met his, her face softened. "I won't forget last night," she whispered. "I really, uh—" She swallowed and spread her hands in a helpless gesture. "I just wanted you to know."

"Gina." His gut constricted. This sounded like goodbye. He cleared his throat, searching for the right words. His mind blanked. "When will you be in Rome again?"

Whatever she'd been expecting him to say, that wasn't it. Her face clouded, but she managed a smile. "No telling. I never know what my route will be. You know me, open to the highest bidder."

Her tone was light and breezy, but she didn't fool him. Especially since he was feeling pretty lousy, too. He cleared his throat again. "Did you want some tea?"

"Uh, no thanks. You said you have my passport?"

He pushed away from his desk so quickly, he almost rolled into his credenza. Instead, he merely scratched his black leather chair on the corner as he swung out of it and went to her.

Gina's eyes widened as he pulled her to her feet, and she let out a low shriek. "Someone could walk in here."

"I don't give a damn," he said, and lowered his mouth to hers.

Her lips softened immediately, her hands clutching the lapels of his jacket, and she clung to him in a way that was immensely reassuring.

Letting go of her wrists, he put his arms around her. She released her death grip on his lapels and looped her arms around his neck. Her breasts crushed against his chest, her heart pounding in time with his, and he didn't know how he was going to ever let her go.

Common sense told him this infatuation would pass. That was the best way he could describe this feeling he was experiencing. They hardly knew each other. How long had it been since he'd met her? Three, four days? How could he justify making any demands or plans at this point?

But kissing her was messing with his head, rendering him incapable of making a conscious decision. He deepened the kiss before slowly pulling back.

Her eyes were dazed and moist, her breathing erratic. His blood pounded in his ears, and he just couldn't seem to let his hands fall from her.

The door opened, and they both turned in slow motion before breaking apart.

Greta's somber gaze swept Gina, then him. "I knocked," she said. "Twice. Apparently you didn't hear me."

"No problem." Jackson stepped farther back and adjusted his tie. "I was just telling Ms. Hart—"

He stopped at the look the two women gave him. Gina looked like a big-eyed wounded doe. Greta, on the other hand, looked as though she wanted to use his tie to string him from the ceiling.

He snorted in self-deprecation. He wasn't fooling a damn soul, least of all himself. Reaching out, he captured Gina's hand. She stiffened for an instant before she let her fingers lightly curl around his. He gave her a reassuring smile, then met Greta's watchful gaze and was amazed to find a hint of approval lurking in her eyes.

Or maybe he wasn't so surprised. She hadn't exactly tried to keep them apart for the past few days, he suddenly realized as suspicion churned in his head and produced a dull ache near his left temple.

"Have you talked with the police?" he asked Greta. "Everything straightened out?"

She nodded. "The charges have been dropped," she said, turning to Gina. "And I trust you have your new passport. So, there's nothing keeping you here." Greta lifted a brow at him. "Unless you know of something, Jackson?"

After a brief but awkward silence, Gina let go of his hand and moved toward Greta. "Thank you so much for all you've done," she said, ignoring the hand Greta extended and hugging the startled receptionist.

Greta squeezed Gina's shoulders right before they parted. "You have a safe trip, and don't be a stranger. You have my home phone number, right?"

"Yup, and I know the embassy's exchange by heart."

Greta laughed as she started for the door. "I hope you only need it for a social call."

"Oh, and your dress is at the cleaners. Isabella will

pick it up when it's ready." A faint blush started at Gina's neck and blossomed in her cheeks. "There's a matter of a small tear to be repaired, but the cleaners assured me they can handle it."

Jackson had sudden recall of the exact moment that dress had torn. In the corridor, outside of his apartment, just as they were...

"Thanks for stopping by, Greta," he said, and finished walking her to the door. Gina would be leaving in a matter of an hour. He didn't want to spend another second talking about some damn dress. "I'll let you know if we need anything."

Greta's lips curved in a knowing smile. "Good luck, Gina. Have a safe trip," she said, and disappeared.

He turned to find Gina eyeing him suspiciously. "You haven't given me my passport yet," she said, and folded her arms across her chest.

"I'm riding with you to the airport."

Her eyes widened, filling with panic, and her arms slipped from their defensive position. "No, you're not."

"We'll have some lunch first. There's this great bistro around the corner—"

"You had a delivery today," she said suddenly, interrupting him. "A chair. It matches the other one in the living room."

Taken aback by the non sequitur, he stopped a couple of feet away from her. Slowly, he nodded. "I was expecting it."

"Yeah, well, I just thought I'd tell you it got there safely."

Although her words were casual, her expression and stance were not. There was an agenda behind her statement, its importance made plain by the anxiety in her gaze, the lines of tension around her mouth. What could she possibly know about the damn chair?

"Thanks. Now, about lunch..."

Disappointment descended upon her face so swiftly her eyes fluttered closed for a moment, and when they opened again, the usual sparkling brown had dulled to the color of autumn mud.

"I can't hang around any longer," she said. "I need to just go. Please understand."

He fumbled with the knot in his tie, wondering what it was he was supposed to understand. "Sure," he finally said, then slowly went to retrieve her passport. Was he supposed to beg her? He wasn't going to do that. Not if she didn't want to stay.

Anger had him roughly jerking her passport from his desk and handing it to her, and he noted with both alarm and satisfaction that her hands were trembling.

"Who do I pay for this?" she asked.

"I've taken care of it."

"No. Absolutely not." She started rooting through her purse until he took one of her cold hands and sandwiched it between his.

"Why are we doing this?" he asked, his anger subsiding in the wake of her nervous fidgeting.

"Doing what?" She raised wary eyes to his.

"Acting like last night was a mistake. Is that the way you feel?"

She shook her head, and for a moment he was afraid she was going to cry. Then she lifted her chin. "I don't have a single regret."

"Me, neither." He smiled, believing her, feeling relieved. "When will I see you again?"

"Officially?" She laughed softly. "I'm sticking this passport in my bra."

"Gina," he said, his tone a mild warning.

"The thing is, Jackson, you have your life and I have mine, and—"

"What's your point?"

Her flip attitude had triggered his anger again, and he struggled to keep it in check. Had he read her so wrong? No, he didn't think so. Maybe she was waiting for him to make some kind of declaration. But he didn't know what to say. That maybe he was just a little in love with her. They'd known each other a mere four days. She'd only laugh. And why not? The idea that love entered into the equation *was* laughable.

She stared at him with troubled eyes, and he felt like a jerk for snapping at her. Normally he didn't have difficulty expressing himself. He had no idea what the hell was wrong.

"I'll call," she said finally.

He hadn't begged so far. Asking when would be pushing it. "Okay." He cleared his throat. They weren't going to be having lunch together. She'd made up her mind. He already knew that, so he wasn't going to bring it up again. "I'll have the car brought up front and we can leave for the airport now if you want."

Her lips curved in a small, sad smile. "I'd rather say goodbye here."

"Why?"

"Because it's easier. Besides, it looks like you have your hands full." She glanced at the chaos on his desk.

"Screw work," he said. "I want to go with you."

His uncharacteristic outburst annoyed him, until he saw something that looked like hope flicker in her eyes.

"I promise I'll call." She laid a hand on his arm.

He hesitated. "When?"

"As soon as I return to New York."

He nodded, trying to find satisfaction in having at least pinpointed a time. But he wanted her to call tomorrow. Hell, he wanted to hear her voice the minute her plane hit Swiss soil.

"Godspeed, Gina," he whispered, then pulled her toward him.

She came willingly, her mouth eagerly meeting his, and he kissed her long and hard, letting his passion speak the words he lacked. Gina didn't hold back, either. She held him like she didn't want to let him go, clinging to him with a desperation that heightened his hopes. When they finally parted, her eyes were moist.

"I really have to go," she said, sniffing and averting her gaze. "I hate goodbyes. I mean, I *really, really* hate them. I get all snappy, which makes me mad, and then I get a horrible headache. Which makes me unfit to live with. And, well, it's not a pretty picture...."

He had to smile at her babbling. It reassured him that she wasn't walking away unscathed. Then he blinked, sobered when his thoughts took a wild turn.

"I doubt you'd be unfit to live with," he said slowly. "Maybe you should let me be the judge of that."

"What are you saying?" she asked with equal caution.

He wasn't sure. He wanted to be with her all the time, there was no question about that. What that meant in the long run, he didn't know. He had his career to think about, and to be honest, he owed Miranda a good long talk. Sucking in a breath, he only stared back at Gina's wary face, once again words failing him.

She smiled, leaned forward and kissed his cheek. "See you around, Jackson."

He watched her walk out the door, heard the soft click of the lock. He didn't know how long he stood there, confused, angry with her for being so composed, but angry mostly with himself for not having the guts to express himself.

When he went to the window, she was already getting into the limo, and all he glimpsed was the swing of her long legs into the back seat. Long after the sleek black car pulled away from the curb and disappeared into traffic, he stood at the window, staring blindly, alone with his stubborn pride.

GINA PICKED UP the receiver, brought it to her ear, then quickly replaced the phone in its cradle as if it were a hot casserole dish and she'd forgotten to use a pot holder. Behind her, someone angrily rattled off something in Italian. She didn't recognize the words, but it wasn't hard to figure out that the woman wanted Gina to get out of line already. This was the third time in a row she'd aborted her attempt to call Jack.

The woman shrieked again, even managing to drown out the loud airport intercom system. Several people grumbled that they'd missed the announcement.

"All right, lady, keep your shirt on," Gina said, and kicked her luggage to the side so that she could move out of the woman's way.

She sighed at her own obnoxious reaction. Just another shining example of how you could take the girl out of Brooklyn, but God forbid you could knock the Brooklyn attitude out of the girl. Jackson would never have yelled at someone to keep their shirt on. He probably would have apologized for having taken up so much time, or at the least kept his ill temper to himself.

That's why she wasn't going to call him. They were oil and water, north and south, vanilla and chocolate. It was better that she was leaving. She finished kicking the luggage to a bank of seats and sank into a blue plastic chair. Hell, this was bad. Not even chocolate sounded good to her right now.

She stared at the line to the phone. Three impatient people glanced sporadically at their watches while they waited for the short woman with the loud pink dress to complete her call.

Their parting today hadn't gone at all like Gina had pictured it. The naive little girl in her, the one who still believed in fairy tales, expected him to beg her to stay, to profess his undying love, to convince her everything would work out. The practical adult side of her had simply wanted him to hold her, kiss her, maybe even suggest a little ongoing affair.

Which proved exactly how far she'd sunk, how pathetic she'd become that she'd be willing to accept crumbs. She sniffed, irritated to find her eyes starting to well up. It was the damn chair that had set her off. So, everything hadn't always been handed to Jackson on a silver platter. And once again she'd misjudged him. Unfortunately, however, she hadn't misjudged his willingness to explain about the loss of the Covington legacy and his struggle to reclaim it.

Didn't he trust her with the truth? Or could he not stand slipping from atop the pedestal for even a minute? Maybe he simply didn't think she was worthy of knowing about that part of his life. Or maybe he thought she'd latch onto that chapter and believe they had enough in common to make a go of things.

Frankly, she had. For just an instant. Before she remembered he wanted to be consul general. And after all, she'd only been a one-night stand for him.

The nastiness of her thoughts shamed her. He wasn't like that. She knew he didn't regard her so carelessly, although she wasn't sure where she stood, either. Sometimes she'd thought she'd actually seen love in his eyes, she'd almost believed that in his own crazy way he'd been trying to ask her to stay, but it was only that little girl in her, wanting the fairy tale. The whole thing was a lie. One her vulnerable psyche had made up in self-defense because she'd done something so incredibly stupid like fall in love with him. She knew that.

That didn't stop her from replaying the last picture she had of him in her head—those blue eyes that never failed to make her knees weak, the tender way he looked at her that made her heart stop altogether. She smiled. The boring red-striped tie.

She was going to have to talk to him eventually. She owed him money. For the dress, for the passport, for a lot of incidentals. And she didn't have his full address. Of course she needed that.

She drummed her fingers on the plastic armrest. Plus, she needed to call him to find out about the charges against her. Sure, Greta said everything had been handled, but as a responsible adult, surely Gina ought to question her exact status with the Italian police.

Her palms started to itch, and she realized they'd grown damp. Only two people stood in line for the pay phone. Her flight wouldn't leave for another half hour. She glanced at her luggage. It wasn't necessary to bring the bags along. She could see them from the phone.

She rose, telling herself she had every reason in the world to call him. This was business. She hated owing anyone money. And she really should have taken care of getting the information before she'd left, but she'd been too rattled.

By the time she filed in line, one person remained ahead of her. After five minutes it was her turn. She picked up the receiver and dropped in several coins.

She hung up before she even got a dial tone.

Chapter Sixteen

Greta picked up the stack of folders Jackson had left for her on the corner of his desk. She stared at him for a long, uncomfortable moment, then said, "Call her."

He stopped twirling his pen between his fingers. "Who?"

"Don't be an ass." After briefly inspecting the label, she moved the top folder to the bottom. "You'll feel better, then maybe you'll get some work done around here."

He glared at her. "She only left two days ago. She's probably still in Switzerland, and I don't know how to get hold of her." He raised a menacing brow. "That is, if I intended to call, which I don't."

Greta shook her head. "I would never have guessed you could be so dense."

Jackson's irritation faded into a resigned sigh, and he stared hard at his old friend. "You did this...pushed us together."

A ghost of a smile played at the corners of Greta's mouth. "You're perfect together."

"Right."

She shrugged, and with an annoying smirk, strolled out the door. He didn't detain her by asking why she thought they were perfect. He didn't want to know. He wanted to be left alone.

He threw aside his pen, picked up his phone and hit Marcy's extension. "I haven't had any calls, have I?" he asked as soon as she answered.

Despite her attempt to conceal it, he heard her impatient sigh. "No," she said, "I'm putting everything through. Just like you told me to do. Twice."

"Right." He barely remembered to mumble a thanks before hanging up. But he did remember. No more taking anyone for granted. At his age, it was a shame he'd needed Gina to remind him of that.

He stared at his Rolodex and wondered if her family knew where she was staying in Switzerland. He had a perfectly legitimate reason to call her. She'd probably want to know how the final police report recounted her status.

Drumming his fingers on his desk, he blew out a stream of air. Even if they didn't know where she was, they'd probably hear from her soon and they could at least give her a message.

A pithy four-letter word came to mind, but he bit it back and picked up the phone. The connection seemed to take forever before a young man with a pronounced Brooklyn accent answered.

Gina wasn't home yet. No, he hadn't heard from her. Sure, he'd give her a message.

By the time Jackson hung up, he wasn't sure if he felt better or worse for having placed the call. Now Gina would know he was sitting here like a damn fool, thinking about her, when here he was, so totally backlogged with work the staff was beginning to whisper about him.

He shook his head. Greta was right. He was an ass. For letting pride stand in his way. Gina might not have said she loved him in so many words, but her eyes told him she did. Besides, he hadn't expressed himself, either. But he missed her, damn it. He missed the sound of her laughter, the way she wouldn't let him take himself so seriously. He missed those long, beautiful legs of hers, especially now that he knew how they felt wrapped around him. He missed the way her hair caught the light and turned to polished bronze.

He scrubbed at his weary eyes, passed a hand over his face. He just plain missed *her*. But did that mean he loved her?

GINA STARED AT THE PHONE for nearly five minutes before she threw herself back on the bed and stared at the hotel ceiling in total, incredulous exasperation. She was acting like a high school sophomore. Besides, it wasn't as though the darn phone was going to ring. He didn't even know where she was.

So why didn't she just pick up the phone and call? She'd been dying to hear his voice since she'd left Rome two days ago. And she'd already mentally cataloged a dozen legitimate reasons to call without sounding like a lovesick puppy. So why didn't she just do it?

Because Switzerland was still too close to Rome, and if he sounded the least bit interested, she'd be running back to him like a mindless twit, that's why.

She rolled over onto her side and stared at the phone again. As soon as she found out her package was ready for transport she could call. They'd said the delay should be no more than a day.

Oh, hell.

She struggled to a sitting position and took several deep breaths. She could do this. She could make a simple call without falling to pieces, or hopping a plane like an obsessed, hormone-driven teenager.

Besides, if she wanted a decent night's sleep, she *had* to do this.

Her hand trembled as she picked up the phone, and she was tempted to slam it back down. But instead, she calmly recited the number she knew by heart to the operator and waited for the connection, her heart pounding so hard her ears started to ring, and half hoping he wouldn't be there. If she left a message, how quickly he returned her call would tell her something.

She shook her head at her pathetic train of thought. Not even in high school had she been this neurotic.

Catching her haggard reflection in the mirror, she straightened self-consciously as soon as the connection was made. Expecting to hear Marcy's voice, words failed Gina when Jack answered on the second ring.

"Yes," he repeated. "Covington here."

She breathed deeply, then said, "Lighten up, Jack. It's rude to bite a person's head off before you even know who it is."

"Gina?" He laughed. It was a short, startled, delighted sound that made her heart sing. "God, Gina, that was fast."

So much for her burst of euphoria. He wasn't happy to hear from her. He thought she was being a pain in the rear and calling too soon.

"Gina?"

"Yes." She tried to sound more formal this time, disguising the real reason she'd called. "About those charges—"

"How was your trip?"

"Fine. I even managed to hang on to my passport."

He laughed again. "I ran into Diana Frost this morn-

ing. She was sorry she didn't get to have lunch with
you before you left. I told her she'd have another opportunity.''

Gina scooted back on the bed, dragging the phone
with her. "Oh?"

He paused. "Yeah, I told her you might even swing
by here before you head back for New York."

She wrinkled her nose. He got an A-plus for confus-
ing the hell out of her. "Why would I do that?" she
asked slowly, refusing to hope. Then when he didn't
answer right away, another thought occurred to her and
she sagged against the headboard. "Have the police re-
instated the charges against me?"

"No. Why would you think that?" Silence. "I miss
you."

"You do?"

"Of course I do." He sounded irritated. "So does
Isabella."

"Oh. Tell her I miss her, too. She really is a sweetheart."

There was another silence, as if he expected her to
say more. Finally, he asked, "So, do you think you'll
be swinging by here?"

"Not a chance. My pickup has been delayed, and the
company who hired me is champing at the bit back in
New York."

"Maybe next time."

"Sure." She twisted the phone cord around her fingers. He'd said he missed her. Was he just being polite?
Should she admit she missed him, too?

"I may be in New York soon."

"Really? On business?"

"Vacation."

She didn't remember him mentioning that before, and

her pulse quickened. "Maybe I'll see you," she said casually.

"Plan on it."

She smiled and snuggled into the pillows. "Do you know when you'll be there?"

"Not at this point. Do you have an itinerary for the next few weeks? Maybe you should give me some alternative numbers where I can reach you."

"I don't know where I'll be," she said truthfully. "I'll know more when I get back to New York."

"Okay." He sounded as though he didn't believe her. "Then should I just leave word with your brother again?"

"My brother? When did you talk to my brother?"

"I figured he was the one who took my message."

"Your message?" She grinned. Jack had left her a message. "Oh, yeah. That'll be fine. You can always call him."

Someone knocked at the door, and as tempted as she was to ignore the person, she figured it was news about her pickup. "Jack? I gotta go."

"Gina?" he said, his tone urgent.

At the same time, she said, "I missed you, too."

She heard the smile in his voice as he said, "Take care, okay? But if you lose your passport, I know the Swiss consul general."

She laughed. "That ain't gonna happen. I'll call again, okay?"

"Okay," he said, then paused. He had something more to say. Gina could hear his hesitation in the suffocating silence.

The knock at the door became more insistent. "Jack, there's somebody here. I really have to go."

"Goodbye, honey," he whispered.

Honey? Her insides melted. "See you," she said, and calmly replaced the phone. Rolling off the bed, she nearly tripped on the tangled comforter. She ran to the door, grabbed her message from the bellhop and tipped him generously. Then she raced back to the phone and called her brother.

JACKSON TOYED WITH the corner of his address book. In the interest of getting one scrap of work done, he had to call her brother again. He'd been foolish in not insisting on getting her hotel phone number, or pinning her on a day she'd call back. It had only been a week since he'd talked to her, but each day was a major test of his patience.

The apartment seemed empty and quiet, although between him and Isabella, fresh flowers continued to grace each room. Not that he needed the reminder of Gina. He missed her with an ache so deep he would never have guessed the intensity possible. He missed her sparkling eyes, the small, thoughtful ways she lavished kindness. He missed the contentment he felt when he was with her.

He didn't even care about the furniture anymore. The chair he'd received the day Gina left continued to sit where Isabella had unwrapped it.

Jackson picked up the phone and dialed before he chickened out. Lots of things amazed him these days. Like his appalling lack of courage when it came to expressing himself to Gina.

She answered on the first ring, and expecting to get her brother, Jack stuttered over her name.

Gina laughed. "Jack? Is that you?"

"No, Hugh Grant."

She laughed again, sounding so delighted he relaxed and grinned.

"I was just about to call you," she said. "We must be on the same wavelength."

"You were?"

"Yes, I'd forgotten to ask you for an address. I'm sending you a check today."

He hesitated, then decided he had to quit being so spineless. "Is that the only reason you were going to call?"

The silence stretched for so long, he figured he wasn't going to like her answer. "No," she said finally.

He exhaled. "Why, then, Gina?"

"I, uh, know what my schedule is for next month."

Insecurity thinned her voice, and Jackson frowned. That wasn't like Gina. She was impulsive and mouthy, not insecure. He scrubbed at his eyes, exhaustion washing over him. He was such a damned fool. He knew where her wariness was coming from. The same place his was. They'd both done nothing but tap-dance. It was up to him to put an end to this.

"Good. I hope Rome is on the list," he said, discovering pride had a most unpleasant aftertaste. "I have plans for this very special dinner."

"Oh, isn't Greta or Miranda available?"

"Miranda and I had a long talk. We won't be going to any more dinners together. Besides, I had a more private dinner in mind."

Her silence did not reassure him. Finally, she said, "I don't know, Jackson."

"Why not?"

She hedged. "It just might not work out."

"I'll send you a ticket if that's the problem."

"The problem is, Jack," she said, her voice rising,

"I'm a working girl. I have bills to pay, responsibilities to meet. I can't just fly off at a moment's notice just because you snap your fingers and produce a plane ticket for me."

It would serve no purpose to get angry, he told himself. "I'll ignore the fact that you're implying I don't have such responsibilities," he said evenly. *Snap my fingers, hell.* "If you recall, I'd asked what your schedule is so we could work around it."

She sighed. "We'll talk about it later. I'm still exhausted from this last trip."

"Fair enough." It wasn't fair at all. He missed her. Probably too much.

Gina had once accused him of being born with a silver spoon. She'd looked at all the material things he'd collected throughout his life, and she thought he had it all. He shook his head as they ended their conversation and he hung up the phone. She was so wrong. He didn't have her.

IT HAD BEEN THREE WEEKS and four days since she'd seen Jack, and Gina was having a serious case of withdrawal. Talking on the phone every other day was nice, but it didn't count. It made her miss him even more. And her phone bill. Forget about it. She'd already told her brother to pay it out of her account while she was on her next trip and not tell her what the damages were. Although she wouldn't regret a penny of it.

Jack's bill had to be worse. For some reason he often managed to call her before she had a chance to call him, and she suspected he was trying to save her the expense.

Although it was hard trying to maintain a relationship by phone, she was proud of herself. She'd stuck to her guns and stayed away from Rome. Even though she'd since had a trip to Paris. But she'd decided that she couldn't be within arm's reach. How did she know their relationship wasn't purely physical?

There were so many differences between them, this was the only way she knew to test the water. They had already had several disagreements, and they'd both lost their temper to some degree, but they had managed to reason things out. And as a result, she felt closer to him.

She'd learned a lot about him, too, things she may have never known had they spent their time in bed instead of talking. One thing that surprised her was that he liked motorcycles and kept one in a garage in Rome, although he admitted that he worked too hard and had let too many weekends go by without taking it for a spin.

She also learned that he liked kids, that he wanted three, and at least one had to be a boy. She smiled, remembering his certainty. Then she groaned, recalling how she'd dreamed that same night how she'd given birth to triplets. Funny, she really hadn't thought much about children or worried that her time was running out, but she did now. And that admittedly bothered her.

He still hadn't told her about the furniture yet, about how he was still buying back everything his father had lost at the gaming tables, and that remained a thorn in her side, but she wasn't exactly hinging anything on it. She just wished he trusted her with the information, even though it didn't really change anything.

She glanced at her watch, carefully trying to keep the towel wrapped around her wet hair from coming free. It was eight in the evening Rome time. Jack would be home now. She smiled and reached for the phone, but before she could pick up the receiver, it rang.

"Jack?"

He laughed. "When I lived in the States, it was customary to say hello when you answered a phone."

"Oh, damn it."

"Times really have changed."

"Sorry. I kicked over a bottle of nail polish."

"Come and Get Me Pink?"

She choked out a laugh. "Excuse me?"

"You were wearing that color the first day you came to the embassy."

"I assure you I have no polish by that name."

"Pity. That color made me hornier than a bull in heat," he said, then added something graphic and very undiplomatic.

"Jack." She laughed. By now she wasn't surprised he had a wild streak in him that belied the diplomatic image. It was all those years of boarding school discipline, he'd told her. He was still rebelling. She smiled at the thought as she pulled the towel off her hair and tried to tame the flyaway wisps that had dried too soon.

"Today I let it be known to the powers that be that I may be ready for a transfer."

Gina straightened and nearly kicked the polish over again. "Can you do that? I mean, and still be considered for the consul general's position?"

"Sure. Although, I'm having second thoughts about that, too."

"Did you tell them that?"

"No, I wasn't that blunt. I just said I needed some time stateside."

Gina's heart throbbed painfully. *Stateside.* He'd said stateside. "But what about all your beautiful antiques? You'll have to move them."

Jack grunted. "Somehow, I expected a different reaction. Anyway, I'm certainly not going to base a decision on a bunch of old furniture.''

"Old furniture?'' She laughed, sounding nervous. She hoped he didn't notice. "They're called antiques, Jackson, and don't they belong to your family?'' She already knew they did, and how much they meant to him.

"They're mine now.'' He hesitated, and she held her breath, waiting for him to reveal some deep, dark secret. "I've only had those pieces for several years. Some of them only for a matter of months. I bought them back as I could afford them. My father gambled everything away long ago.''

"Oh,'' she said, yanking at the phone cord. She already knew that, too, but he was so blasé it irritated her. She'd waited a long time for him to share this with her. Obviously she'd placed too much importance on it. "I'm sorry.''

"No need to be. In college, I thought it was the end of the world,'' he admitted. "Now I consider the experience character building.''

"Did you wait tables in college?'' she asked suddenly, remembering that night in his kitchen.

"I was tip king,'' he said proudly. "Always made more than anyone else.''

She still had so much to learn. "I bet all your customers were ladies.''

"Hey, I earned those tips.'' He laughed. "Wouldn't you rather talk about my moving to New York?''

"New York? This New York?'' She'd assumed he'd meant D.C. New York meant something else entirely. She hoped she had something to do with his decision.

"You have a problem with that?''

"Jack? What kind of job would you do here?''

"You sound disappointed."

She was stunned. And she was trying not to hope. "This isn't what you wanted."

"Things and times change, Gina. Priorities change. I want to be close to you."

A moment of silence passed. "You big dope." She sniffed, still not sure what this all meant, but letting hope fill her, anyway. "You have no business telling me this stuff on the phone. I was planning on surprising you and coming to Rome this weekend." She glanced at the navy blue suit hanging on the door she'd bought just this morning for the occasion. She hadn't needed to think twice about the conservative purchase as she would have two months ago. Jack had never asked her to change. She knew he never would. "This is the kind of news you tell someone in person."

"I was hoping you'd say that. Look out your window, Gina."

"What?" She blinked and slowly twisted around in her chair. She didn't see anything unusual at first, other than the regular late afternoon traffic.

And then she saw him. Across the street, at a pay phone. He stepped out of the glass cubicle to wave, and she heard horns blaring through the phone line.

She dropped the receiver and scrambled to pick it up again. She hadn't shaved her legs in two days. Her hair was still damp and sticking out in every direction, and she was wearing her brother's ratty gray sweatshirt.

Breathless, she pulled the receiver to her mouth. "Don't you dare come up now."

"I'm touched by your enthusiasm."

"Give me a half hour," she said, unable to tear her gaze from him. It looked as though he had on jeans.

She'd never seen him in those before. "I don't have any makeup on."

He laughed. "Do you know how many times I've seen you without it?" he asked, and when she started to balk, he said, "I used to watch you sleep."

She swallowed, knowing she'd analyze that little tidbit of information later. "You still can't come up now."

"Forget it. Open up or I'm breaking the door down."

She giggled. "You wouldn't—"

The dial tone stopped her cold. She let the phone drop to the floor and she stared out the window, watching him as he looked both ways for traffic, then jogged across the street toward her apartment.

Her thoughts froze. *She* froze. How could she let him see her like this? She flew off the chair and started for the bathroom, stopped and went to her bedroom instead. As she caught a glimpse of herself in her dresser mirror, her heart pounded more frantically. She looked like hell. And here she'd been worried about him seeing a little cellulite.

Forcing herself to slow her breathing, she picked up a brush and ran it through her hair. Static crackled, making her hair stick out with greater enthusiasm. She shook her head and heard the knock at the same time.

Sheesh, she'd wanted to test the relationship, but this was definitely not what she had in mind.

At another insistent knock, she smoothed down the old sweatshirt, held her head up and went to open the door.

Jack looked great. As soon as his anxious blue eyes met hers, a smile broke out across his face that made her forget she looked like a bum. "Gina."

"Hi." A wave of inexplicable shyness washed over her, and she tightened her hold on the knob for support.

Uncertainty flickered in his eyes, dimmed his smile. "I respect your need for space and I promise I won't crowd you. I'm only here for the weekend."

His hesitancy touched her. Jack was always confident. Yet he hadn't taken her reaction for granted. He didn't assume she'd be grateful for his attention. He'd come halfway around the world with his heart on his sleeve and he was asking her to accept him.

"Don't you dare not crowd me." She grabbed a handful of his black polo shirt and pulled him to her.

His arms automatically came up to hug her, his heartfelt sigh filling her ears and soul. His body was warm and solid, and she knew this time she wouldn't be able to stay away. Ever.

He pulled back. "You look beautiful."

"Yeah, right." That lie deserved a good hard smack, but instead she backed them up into her apartment and let him shut the door behind them.

He kissed the tip of her nose, then purposefully met her gaze and held it. "Love does that. Make everything look rosy."

Emotion burst like a display of fireworks in her heart. "Damn it, Jackson." She punched his arm. "You can't always say the right things. It isn't fair."

He laughed softly, then kissed her. It was a brief, unsatisfying kiss, but she could tell he was holding back. "You're wrong. I don't always say the right things. But I'm trying to make up for it now." He kissed her again, then gazed steadily at her. "I love you, Gina Hart. Probably more than I have a right to."

She moistened her lips. "Not if I love you back."

He smiled and held her close for a moment. Then he pulled away again to look at her and asked, "Do you?"

She nodded. "Probably more than I have a right to."

"Why?"

She blinked, surprised by his seriousness. "We're really different, you know."

A thoughtful frown lined his forehead. "In some ways, that's true. How boring life together would be otherwise," he said, one corner of his mouth lifting, but Gina was having trouble getting past the word *together* and the hope it inspired. "But not in the ways that matter. Besides, I've never learned anything from being exposed to what I already know, have you?"

"What could I teach you, Jackson?" she asked.

"Is that your bedroom over there?" he asked in turn, nudging his chin over her shoulder.

"Hey, that's not what I meant."

Chuckling, he started backing her up. "You've taught me a lot, Gina, trust me. And as much as I'd love to tell you I'm old-fashioned and can wait for the wedding, that ain't gonna happen."

She arched her brows. "I'm shocked at your language. *Ain't?* They teach you that at boarding school?"

He grinned, and she remembered using the term once or twice herself. So, she had taught him something, she thought, laughing.

She sobered.

Wedding? He'd said wedding. "What wedding?"

The bed hit the backs of her legs and she sank down, her bottom hitting the mattress with an ungraceful thud.

Jack dropped to one knee. "Our wedding. I hope." He started to dig into his jeans pocket, but he was having so much trouble she saw the outline of the small square box pressed against the denim before he withdrew it.

She started laughing and threw her arms around his

neck, hindering him further. "And here I thought you were just happy to see me. Yes, I'll marry you."

"I didn't ask you yet," he grumbled, still trying to free the box with one hand while hugging her with the other.

It didn't matter. She'd made up her mind to love him well before he'd asked. He was right. They shared the same views on everything that mattered. And with him, Gina knew she would always feel special.

Jackson wrestled with trying to withdraw the ring box for another few seconds before he gave up and crawled up on the bed to stretch out beside Gina. She didn't care about the ring or how big it was. Gina loved him and not the material things with which he could provide her.

He did have to get a ring on her finger pretty damn quick, though, he thought as she wrapped her arms round him and pressed her lips to his. They had three beautiful babies to make.

Epilogue

Two months later

Dear Libby and Jessie,

Okay, you guys, I know I'm pond scum for not writing sooner, but so much has happened in the past few months I don't even know where to begin.

I lied. I know exactly where to begin. Are you two sitting down?

Ahem. (That was me taking a deep breath.)

Okay. Are you ready?

I'm married!

Go ahead and blink, sputter, cough. But I really am married. Yes, me, Gina Marie Hart... Covington. His name is Jackson Maxwell Covington III, by the way. But trust me, he's not prissy like his name sounds. Besides, can you imagine me married to anyone prissy? I don't think so.

Honestly, he's the nicest, greatest, most patient man in the world. He's got a few bucks in the bank, too, but I don't hold that against him.

Anyway, we met in Rome, at the American Embassy after I got my wallet and passport ripped off. He's one of the assistant consuls here in Rome, but by the time you get this letter we'll probably be headed back for New York where he's been reassigned.

I really wish you could have come to the wedding, but things happened so fast after he proposed that I didn't have time to invite anyone, much less plan anything elaborate. Now, I know what you're thinking, and no, I'm not pregnant. Tell that to my family, though. When we decided to get married ASAP, my moronic brothers pulled out calendars and threatened to kick poor Jack's butt if I started ballooning up too soon. But that's another story.

But don't get me wrong...all the Harts are crazy about Jackson. Actually, all the Harts are plain crazy, but that's another story, too.

Okay, back to the details...we got married two months ago, several days after Jack came to visit me in New York, and then returned to Rome with him. I'm still working a few courier jobs, but embassy dinners and such keep me busy, too.

I know, I know. You're gagging at this point. But it isn't so bad. I've met lots of interesting people...some blowhards, too, but I ignore them. I'm also learning how to ride a motorcycle and how to swear in six different languages.

Only kidding about the swearing. But I am taking French and German, and I'm seriously thinking about going back to school for my teaching certificate. Jack thinks that would be great, but of course, he thinks anything I want to do is great. What can I say? The guy is crazy about me. (Picture me sitting here with a big sappy grin.)

Okay, kiddos, enough about me. What's going on with you two? Write when you can and tell all.

I miss you both. Maybe we can get together for a gabfest soon?

Love,
Gina

P.S. Remember our Trevi Fountain wishes? The boy said only one wish would come true—my wish didn't. Good thing, too, 'cause Sister Gina doesn't have such a nice ring to it! Only kidding. Opportunity knocked, and I'm glad I didn't run away. Jackson *is* that one in a million. I can't wait to hear about what happened with your wishes!

Take 2 bestselling love stories FREE

Plus get a FREE surprise gift!

Special Limited-Time Offer

Mail to Harlequin Reader Service®

P.O. Box 609
Fort Erie, Ontario
L2A 5X3

YES! Please send me 2 free Harlequin American Romance® novels and my free surprise gift. Then send me 4 brand-new novels every month, which I will receive months before they appear in bookstores. Bill me at the low price of $3.71 each plus 25¢ delivery and GST*. That's the complete price, and a saving of over 10% off the cover prices—quite a bargain! I understand that accepting the books and gift places me under no obligation ever to buy any books. I can always return a shipment and cancel at any time. Even if I never buy another book from Harlequin, the 2 free books and the surprise gift are mine to keep forever.

354 HEN CH7F

Name	(PLEASE PRINT)	
Address	Apt. No.	
City	Province	Postal Code

This offer is limited to one order per household and not valid to present Harlequin American Romance® subscribers. *Terms and prices are subject to change without notice.
Canadian residents will be charged applicable provincial taxes and GST.

CAMER-98   ©1990 Harlequin Enterprises Limited

THE RANDALL MEN ARE BACK!

Those hard-ridin', good-lovin' cowboys who lassoed
your heart—Jake, Chad, Brett and Pete Randall—are
about to welcome a long-lost kin to their Wyoming
corral—Griffin Randall.

Big brother Jake has married off all of his brothers—
and himself. How long can Griffin escape Jake's
matchmaking reins?

Find out in
COWBOY COME HOME
by Judy Christenberry

*They give new meaning
to the term "gettin' hitched"!*

Available at your favorite retail outlet.

Intense, dazzling, isolated...

THE AUSTRALIANS

Stories of romance Australian-style, guaranteed to
fulfill that sense of adventure!

This October, look for

Beguiled and Bedazzled

by Victoria Gordon

Colleen Ferrar is a woman who always gets what she wants—
that is, until she meets Devon Burns, who lives in the very
secluded Tasmanian bush. He has a proposal of his own, and
the question is: how far will Colleen go to get what she wants?

*The Wonder from Down Under: where spirited women win
the hearts of Australia's most independent men!*

Available October 1998
at your favorite retail outlet.

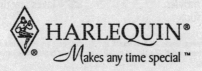

HARLEQUIN®
Makes any time special ™

MEN at WORK

All work and no play?
Not these men!

July 1998

MACKENZIE'S LADY by Dallas Schulze

Undercover agent Mackenzie Donahue's
lazy smile and deep blue eyes were his best
weapons. But after rescuing—and kissing!—
damsel in distress Holly Reynolds, how could
he betray her by spying on her brother?

August 1998

MISS LIZ'S PASSION by Sherryl Woods

Todd Lewis could put up a building with ease,
but quailed at the sight of a classroom! Still,
Liz Gentry, his son's teacher, was no battle-ax,
and soon Todd started planning some
extracurricular activities of his own....

September 1998

A CLASSIC ENCOUNTER
by Emilie Richards

Doctor Chris Matthews was intelligent, sexy
and *very* good with his hands—which made
him all the more dangerous to single mom
Lizette St. Hilaire. So how long could she
resist Chris's special brand of TLC?

Available at your favorite retail outlet!

MEN AT WORK™

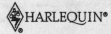 

Look us up on-line at: http://www.romance.net   PMAW2

**SEXY, POWERFUL MEN NEED
EXTRAORDINARY WOMEN WHEN THEY'RE**

*Destined
for
Love*

Take a walk on the wild side this October
when three bestselling authors weave wondrous stories
about heroines who use their extraspecial abilities to
achieve the magic and wonder of love!

HATFIELD AND McCOY
by HEATHER GRAHAM POZZESSERE

LIGHTNING STRIKES
by KATHLEEN KORBEL

MYSTERY LOVER
by ANNETTE BROADRICK

Available October 1998
wherever Harlequin and Silhouette books are sold.

HARLEQUIN®
Makes any time special ™

Silhouette™

Look us up on-line at: http://www.romance.net   PSBR1098